USA TODAY BESTSELLING AUTHOR
NANCY WARREN

CAKES AND PAINS

THE GREAT WITCHES BAKING SHOW
BOOK 8

Ambleside Publishing

INTRODUCTION

Baking and betrayal are a recipe for murder!

Poppy's happy in her new role as baker at Broomewode Inn, exploring her powers as a witch and enjoying the friendship of Benedict Champney. However, when Benedict's father, the Earl of Frome, insists on running a fox hunt, Poppy's outraged. She calms down when she learns they don't use a real fox, just a scented rag for the hounds and hunters to follow, but someone is being hunted. To death.

Meanwhile, Poppy's meeting a woman who she believes once knew her mother and feels she's getting closer to the mystery of her birth. Until the woman disappears.

It's the semi-finals in The Great British Baking Contest and tensions are running high for the three remaining contestants. Who will win? And will Poppy stay alive long enough to find out?

Join Poppy and her friends in this 8th novel in The Great Witches Baking Contest series of paranormal cozy mysteries.

There's humor, quirky characters, a little romance and no bad language or gore. Oh, and recipes!

If you haven't met Rafe Crosyer yet, he's the gorgeous, sexy vampire in *The Vampire Knitting Club* series. You can get his origin story free when you join Nancy's no-spam newsletter at NancyWarrenAuthor.com.

Come join Nancy in her private Facebook group where we talk about books, knitting, pets and life. www.facebook.com/groups/NancyWarrenKnitwits

CAKES AND PAINS

CHAPTER 1

"*H*ow are the madeleines going, Poppy?"

I lifted my head from the bowl and nodded at the new chef. "You were right, Ruta. Adding more brown sugar gives the mix an almost caramel scent."

"After churning out two hundred a day, you learn a thing or two." Ruta flashed me a toothy grin and went back to her prep.

I loved the mornings at Broomewode Inn, even if they were so early as to still feel like the night before. But when the sun began to stream through the glistening windows and skylight, the busy kitchen felt like it was being smiled upon by Mother Nature herself. Since mothers were on my mind at the moment, the idea pleased me. Light bounced off of the immaculate stainless-steel worktops, gas ranges, and fridges, making the space appear even bigger than it was.

Plus, providing the proverbial Maraschino cherry on top was my new boss, head chef Ruta. After the whole village found out about some marital troubles, my old boss couldn't face staying in the village and decided to leave work pronto.

Super quick—like, I've never seen someone change their life so fast. I felt awful for Sol. Not only had he found out that the woman he'd pledged to share his life with was having an affair, but he'd also experienced the whole sorry mess playing out in a pub full of villagers. That was definitely a sour cherry on the top. He was a proud man, and neither he nor his wife wanted to stay after being implicated in murder and deception.

Which brings me back to Ruta, my new boss. Sol didn't leave us completely in the lurch. He made a call to a restaurant he'd once worked at in London and somehow sweet-talked his old sous-chef, who'd replaced him as head chef, into doing the same thing at Broomewode Inn. I didn't know what magic he poured into her ear, but I could sure do with learning the spell. Before you could say alakazam—*poof!* Sol was gone, and there was Ruta—all six feet of her. Broad-shouldered, solid of body, and creamy-skinned, Ruta was as no-nonsense as any chef I'd met but kind and thoughtful too. She didn't let a busy service get her in a temper, and although I'd grown to appreciate Sol's gruff nature, I preferred her less barky style of running the show. She was incredibly skilled and brought with her cutting-edge recipes from London. Within three days, Ruta had added Szechuan peppercorns, sumac, and ancho chilies to the already bulging larder shelves. I had no idea what kind of recipes were percolating in her imagination, but I was excited to try them all. *Time to shake things up in this sleepy village*, she'd said. Ha, if only she knew how much drama went down in Broomewode. Sleepy was so not the right word. With *The Great British Baking Contest* nearing its final episode, there was bound to be plenty of drama this weekend and next.

Best of all, Ruta was fond of cats, and she let me bring Gateau to work so long as she stayed out of the kitchen. My sweet little black cat (and familiar) adored roaming the grounds as I toiled in the kitchen, exhausting herself chasing the butterflies and then sleeping all the way on the drive home to my cottage, curled into a ball on the passenger seat, letting off the odd kittenish snore.

I sifted my flour and began to fold it into my egg and sugar mix, careful not to do too much at a time for fear of letting the air out of my batter. This was my second week on the job at Broomewode Inn, and I still had to pinch myself. If I'd told my ten-year-old self that one day I'd be a pastry chef in a small English village, young Poppy would have giggled in my face. Probably made a rude noise, too. *I'm going to be a famous painter,* I could hear her scoff. *My work will hang in the MoMA.* Hmm, maybe mini me wouldn't have known about the Museum of Modern Art, but she would have wanted me to aim high. But here I was, happier than ever in the kitchen. A huge, gleaming, professional kitchen. I was officially A Pro. I still worked as a graphic artist and illustrator, but that work had become very much a weekend and evening second job.

I took a sip of my coffee (third one this morning, but I needed something to get me through the brutally early mornings). Then, caffeinated up, I poured my madeleine mix into airtight containers, the aroma of brown sugar diffusing through the air. I took the containers to the huge stainless-steel fridges, where they'd sit until someone in the restaurant ordered a batch later this afternoon. It would take just twelve minutes to turn the gooey mix into golden sponge. I was almost jealous of whoever would sample my labors of love.

But there was no time for dwelling on cakes not yet eaten.

I had to get the chocolate fondants prepped for lunch service. The recipe was another one that Ruta had tweaked. She suggested a new Valrhona chocolate (all the flashy London restaurants used it, apparently), and I was always happy to improve. But as I retrieved my ingredients from the overflowing pantry, my mind turned to *The Great British Baking Contest*.

The semifinal was in two days, and Florence, Gaurav, and Hamish were entering chocolate week. Chocolate was a simple enough ingredient, but I knew that judges Elspeth Peach and Jonathon Pine would have cooked up a whole host of tricky signature, technical, and showstopper challenges. My three friends had been texting me all week, Florence in a flurry of messages, one after the other—reminiscent of the breathless way she talked when excited. Hamish more to the point. Gaurav with lots of niceties, worried about bothering me. They'd all been after my advice or approval, but I tried my best to remain impartial. I didn't want to steer them one way or the other. Imagine if I did give some advice in all good faith and then their chocolate delights didn't, well, delight. I wouldn't want to shoulder that responsibility. Besides, I wanted them all to win, so I stuck to offering moral support.

Despite all the communication, not one of my friends told me the exact nature of the tasks they'd been set. It was strange—no, super weird. Normally it was all the competition bakers could talk about. *How could they have set us a challenge with cheesecake—I hate cheese!* Or, *is Jonathon Pine out of his mind thinking we can make babkas?* Each baker had wanted my opinion, but they'd texted me about flavor combinations and sourcing ingredients; texture options and places to buy piping bags. I could never get a handle on exactly what they were making. The intrigue was bizarre. But my week had been full of other pressing matters, so I just put their secrecy down to their collective nerves.

I carried bars of chocolate for the fondants back to my workstation, and Pavel nodded his head shyly as I passed. He was peeling potatoes for a Jerusalem artichoke gratin that was one of the day's specials. With Sol gone, Pavel had become even more quiet—I suspected that being the only man in a kitchen of women made him bashful. With thoughtful Ruta at the helm and shy Pavel as a colleague, Broomewode Inn was a serene place to work. The only inter-ruption—the continual interruption—was Gerry. My dear never-departing ghost pal Gerry, whose favorite new trick was to float through my workstation, curl up beside my blender, and pull faces at me. The first time, I'd leapt back surprised and let go of the lid. Yogurt mix everywhere. Which sent Gerry into full-on fist-pumping delight. He tried to high-five me, which I'd have refused even if there was a hand to smack. He was lucky I was the only one who could hear him —the man sounded like a squealing goat. Gerry really didn't get the ghostly part of being a ghost—you know, the bit about quiet and not being seen.

I weighed the chocolate and then my phone buzzed in the back pocket of my jeans. I fiddled with my apron strings and slid it out.

It was a text from Florence.

Darling Pops, how's it all going being a top prof chef? Sending kisses from the train to Broomewode. Just checking our dearest Susan is keeping some of those glorious happy eggs for me for the all-impor-

tant semifinal? Maybe we can pop to the farm
together on your break? MISS YOU CAN'T WAIT
TO CATCH UP. <3 <3 <3

I laughed. How like Florence to double-check on her
ingredients. I'd already spoken to Susan Bentley during the
week to make sure Florence could bake with her happy eggs
at the weekend. It wasn't as if the eggs were going to suddenly
run out. Susan had plenty to go around, but I did understand
Florence's nerves. Who better than someone who'd also been
a competitor in the reality show? I'd been voted off. Bread
had been my undoing, but I really didn't miss the stress. The
competition was almost at its final stage, and Florence
wanted every advantage possible. And once a person tasted
Susan's eggs, no one could ever go back to ordinary ones.
Susan was a witch, like me, and I sometimes wondered if she
did more than feed her chickens the best food and let them
wander outside.

I dashed off a quick reply and told Florence I was due at
the farm after the morning rush was over to pick up eggs for
the inn anyway. I'd pick up hers at the same time.

A few minutes later, and my phone buzzed again. But this
time, the message was from Hamish.

Hi lassie, I heard that Susan Bentley has some spectacular eggs...any chance of asking for a few
speckled lovelies for your ol' pal Hamish? I could do
with an extra boost this weekend. Nerves are
running high! H

Oh, Florence wouldn't be happy. She thought those eggs

would give her a competitive edge; now she'd be sharing that little extra something with Hamish. I wasn't surprised he'd heard about them. The eggs were spectacular. I was pleased to be bringing Susan more business and asked Hamish if two dozen would see him through the weekend, and he sent back a smiley emoji.

The chocolate was beginning to melt, and I added some unsalted butter to the bowl, stirring until the mix became one glorious shiny liquid that smelled like heaven. I was glad to be free from the cameras that had once followed me around the competition tent as I baked. I couldn't blame Florence and Hamish for wanting to do everything they could to make the weekend go in their favor. To have come as far as the semifinals was a huge achievement—I, too, would want to battle through to try my hand at winning. Along with Gaurav, they must be racked with nerves. I was more than happy to be the one watching from the sidelines.

My phone buzzed again. Luckily Ruta was too engrossed with something bubbling on the stove to notice how much I was getting interrupted. I slipped it from my back pocket and hoped it wasn't a message from Joanna bailing on our arrangement to meet. I'd been trying hard to keep my mind on the job all morning, but other than being Broomewode's official egg dealer, this afternoon I was due to meet a local newspaper editor's daughter named Joanna, who had known my birth mother.

I was so excited, I could hardly stand it. I'd been digging for clues to my parentage ever since I arrived at Broomewode. I was certain that a woman named Valerie, who had worked in the kitchen of Broomewode Hall, was my birth mother. Broomewode was the beautiful Georgian manor house that was home to the Earl of Frome and his family, and where *The Great British Baking Contest* was filmed on the grounds. I was hoping to finally get some answers about who my mom was and her connection to Broomewode Hall, but I was nervous, too, as Joanna hadn't seemed particularly forthcoming when we spoke on the phone last weekend. Still, she'd agreed to meet me and we were having coffee together this afternoon.

But the text wasn't from Joanna. It was Gaurav. Of *course* it was Gaurav. No prizes for guessing what he wanted.

Dear Poppy, I hope you have been keeping well this week. The weather has been beautiful—well, what I've seen of it through my kitchen window! I heard that you can procure some top quality eggs from the local farmer Susan Bentley. If you're going to her farm, would you mind picking me up a dozen or two? I'd be very grateful. Best wishes, Gaurav.

I shot back another quick affirmative message and imagined Susan's delight when she discovered all the baking contestants preferred her eggs.

I finished prepping the individual fondant pots and told Ruta that I was off to the farm to collect the inn's order and tell Susan I needed extras for the weekend.

"Make sure she's got lots for us for tomorrow," Ruta warned. "I'm counting on her."

I was puzzled. "Tomorrow?" Why was Ruta worried about tomorrow?

"It's the hunt, remember?" she said, a little exasperated. "We need to have plenty of options for the hunt teams who aren't invited to the earl's post-hunt breakfast. We're fully booked and then there will be all the walk-ins."

I groaned. I'd put tomorrow's barbaric activity out of my mind. I hated any kind of animal hunting. The prospect of having to feed a bunch of bloodthirsty hunters turned my stomach. It made me want to find my sweet Gateau and swoop her up into a cuddle puddle. The only foxes I'd ever seen were shy and slunk away the minute I spotted them. They looked like small dogs. Who would want to chase down and kill something that looked so sweet? No doubt Susan, with her chickens to worry about, wouldn't agree, but I had made up my mind fox hunting was barbaric, and I wanted nothing to do with it.

However, I would do my job. If I didn't do my usual routine of wishing the cakes well that were going into hunters' mouths, that was my business. I told Ruta I'd check with Susan about tomorrow's order and removed my apron and dusted off the stray clouds of flour that always seemed to decorate my shirt. I was wearing a new wrap blouse in honor of meeting Joanna later, a soft dusky pink which my best friend Gina picked out when I was too panicked to choose. Gina had accompanied me on my shopping mission to the neighboring city of Bath, and we'd turned it into a full girls' day out with shopping, lunch, and cocktails. I'd almost forgotten what it was like to have a normal life. What with the competition, my other job freelancing as a graphic designer and working every spare minute, and trying to solve the mystery of my birth parents...well, there wasn't much time to be a regular twenty-five-year-old. And, as Gina took sooo much pleasure in pointing out, more time and an updated wardrobe might open things up for me to meet "someone."

"Someone?" I'd replied, all innocent, and then swiftly changed the subject.

As I headed out of the kitchen, I waved to Eve, who was busy setting up the bar.

"You off to Susan's, dearie?"

I nodded and held my breath—was I about to get another happy egg request?

"Send my love," Eve said.

I let out a sigh of relief.

"Ooh and tell her we got a delivery of that rosé wine her and Reg like. There's a bottle with her name on it."

I laughed and promised to pass on the delicious message.

"And honey! Make sure you bring back honey for the bar as well as the kitchen."

I nodded. I liked the walk, but I was going to have to get some of the order delivered. I could try using my witchy powers to transport the goods, but I doubted the people of Broomewode would appreciate watching produce dance down the hill by itself. I chuckled, thinking I was getting ahead of myself. I was just learning my craft. If I tried such a spell, no doubt I'd lose my focus and drop everything on the way. No. Much better to trust a delivery van over my witch skills.

CHAPTER 2

Outside, the morning was bright and fresh, and my spirits were up. My gut was telling me that this afternoon's coffee with Joanna was going to yield some new clues about my mom. I felt I was getting close to understanding where I'd come from and why the woman who gave birth to me then left me outside a bakery in a Somerset apple crate.

Things were looking up. Team Poppy was going to finally get some answers. I went to touch my amethyst necklace, but it wasn't there! "Oh no," I groaned aloud. I held up my wrist. No amulet. How could I have forgotten to put those on this morning? I shook my head and then saw Team Poppy's founding member Gateau having a snooze by a blue hydrangea bush. I went to give her a quick stroke. She rolled onto her back at my touch and stuck two little paws out like she was swimming and fell promptly back asleep. "Not quite the guard cat, are we?" I mused, rubbing her fluffy belly.

I set off for Susan's farm, my mind on the afternoon ahead. At Joanna's request, we were meeting at a café in the neighboring village. She said this way we'd have more privacy, as so many people knew her in Broomewode. The request had thrown me a bit. I hoped she wasn't going to tell me something bad about Valerie, something she didn't want the nosy residents of Broomewode to overhear. I'd soon know. I was counting down the hours until I clocked off at three p.m. and could get in my little red Renault and zoom off to meet the woman who might have known my mother.

My feet followed the familiar path to the farm. We were well into June, and the two hundred or so acres of fields surrounding Broomewode Farm looked more luscious than ever. The rolling green fields were vibrant; the flowerbeds on either side of the path had gorgeous blooms tumbling from the rich soil. My namesake flower had grown like wildfire across the wild meadows, and now the green was smattered with luscious reds and the gorgeous blue of cornflowers. I caught a glimpse of Edward, a local man who'd been hired as an undergardener and been promoted to the gamekeeper job. I waved, but he was too far away to see me.

I looked up at the blue sky, hoping to catch a glimpse of the hawk that often appeared. I felt that he was watching out for me, but today I saw nothing more exciting than a few wood pigeons. Maybe it was a good thing the hawk hadn't appeared. He seemed only to show up when danger was imminent. And I was determined to have a normal week. No more murder. This week was about me and Joanna having a very serious tête-à-tête. This week was about resolution.

Before long, Susan's glorious herb garden came into view, and I inhaled its earthy, fresh scent. Behind it, the farmhouse looked gorgeous in the bright sunshine. I wondered if Susan got lonely in such a large building. Now that she was widowed, maybe the place felt empty. Although with Sly around, and her farm and chickens, she had her hands full—that sweet pup had a way of taking up space. I stood for a moment, suddenly contemplative, but any deep thoughts were shattered by a happy bark. From bark to ball in the blink of an eye, Sly bounded over, chasing his red ball, which he rolled toward my feet. He fixed his eyes on the slobbery rubber ball and half-crouched, all ready to run after it.

"Hello, hello!" I called, laughing. "Here I am, your ball servant." I picked up the slippery thing and threw as far as I could and watched Sly as he bounded across the lawn, a blur of black and white.

I made my way to find Susan in her barn. Thursdays and Fridays were busy prep days for her ahead of the Saturday markets, and I imagined she was frenziedly bottling honey and collecting herbs. Busy or not, I was excited to catch up and share news of my upcoming coffee date with Joanna. I didn't have a lot of time, but Susan, like Eve, knew of my search for my mother. I could tell her about my hopes and fears.

I knocked on the huge oak door of the barn and went in. Susan sat at a wide table with tree stumps for legs, her short, curling hair swept away from her forehead with a wide black band. She looked up and smiled. "Ah, Poppy, come in, come in. I was just finishing bottling." She gestured to a tree stump, and I took a seat. The barn smelled fantastic—sweet and rich from the honey but aromatic, too, from Susan's dried herbs hanging in neat green bundles from the rafters.

Susan was wearing a hessian apron over a loose white linen shirt. The apron was covered in splotches of honey, and there were strands of hay in Susan's hair, but she looked as happy as a kid in a candy shop. I told her as much, and she looked pleased. "I love preparing for the weekend markets," she said. "It's the nicest part of the week, knowing that my honey and eggs and herb tonics will be enjoyed in so many homes. And I adore the conversation. I work alone most of the time, so getting to meet new people at the markets is a delight. You meet all sorts, from locals to tourists."

I felt terrible. "I should visit more often. I always mean to."

Susan quickly added, "Nonsense. I always welcome visits from my youngest coven sister, but I'm happy she's busy being a pastry chef extraordinaire. The quality of dessert has certainly gone up at Broomewode Inn. Reg said the tarte tatin he had the other day was the best he'd ever eaten." Reg was a bit of a silver fox, and he and Susan enjoyed a friendship that would probably be more one day.

I shook my head. "I'm pretty sure that's not true, but I appreciate the compliment. Oh, and Eve said to tell you she's got that rosé you both like back in stock."

"And how's the new chef working out?"

I told Susan I'd already learned new techniques from Ruta. "I love how innovative she is. She never takes the easiest route unless the quality of ingredients is so sublime, simplicity is the only option."

Susan raised her eyebrows good-naturedly. "You're starting to sound quite the professional."

I laughed. "I know. I'm as surprised as you!"

Susan handed me three mason jars and asked me to fill the last lot of honey. I took a copper spoon and began to decant the golden, gooey liquid. "So today is a big day. I'm finally meeting Joanna after I work," I said, catching a drip of honey as it ran down the spoon.

"Joanna?"

"The woman who went to school with my birth mom. Remember how Trim, the reporter for the *Broomewode News,* put me in touch with Mavis, an editor at the same paper?"

Susan nodded, although I could see she was already bemused by so many names.

"Well, Mavis had recognized the name Valerie—she was an old school friend of her daughter, Joanna. We made contact last week, and now we're meeting for coffee at The Hourglass."

Susan nodded again but then frowned. She cocked her head to one side and looked up at me. "The Hourglass? Why, that's almost a twenty-minute drive from here. Why are you meeting in Larkville? There are a couple of nice coffee shops here."

I shrugged. I'd been thinking the same thing. "Joanna said she wanted privacy."

Susan looked thoughtful, and she screwed the lids of the mason jars tight before cutting some plaid ribbon with which to secure them. After a minute, she said, "I think it's wonderful you've got a new lead. I just don't want you to get your hopes up too high. You've hit a lot of dead ends in your search, and who knows if this Joanna even remembers your mother. Her school days were a long time ago. Just be...cautious."

I wanted to agree, but cautiousness wasn't in my blood, so I nodded instead. I kicked myself again for forgetting to wear the protective necklace and amulet Elspeth Peach had given me. But I was meeting the daughter of a local newspaper editor. Why on earth would I need protection?

"I suppose it makes sense," Susan was saying. "Larkville is connected to Broomewode, of course. You'll still be on the earl's land. He owns The Hourglass and the flats above it, as well as all the land the dairy farm is on."

"You're kidding," I said, but held my tongue before I complained that the Earl of Frome, Robert Champney, seemed to lord it over everyone. The earl was still an old friend of Susan's late husband *and* her landlord. But it didn't sit right with me that one man should own so much land and have so much wealth only because he'd been born to it. He should spread the wealth around a little. But there was no escaping the earl's fortune. His holdings were vast.

"You must pop into the dairy farm if you get the chance," she said. "I know the farmer, name's Riley. Nathaniel Riley. He's a dreadful man, but his cream and butter are outstanding. There was no love lost between him and my husband. Riley thought we were simply awful city folk. He didn't respect us trying our hand at working the land." She swiftly tied bows on the remaining jars and stood. "I learned not to take it personally. He seems to hate everyone, especially the earl, who's his landlord as well. He'd be happier somewhere like America where there is no aristocracy to contend with. But he's as bound by the past as anyone. His family have been tenant farmers for generations." She rose. "Right. Let's leave the past where it belongs and get your order for the inn sorted."

To me, the past wasn't just the past. I suspected it was the key to my present, but again, I kept quiet. I couldn't expect anyone else to understand. Maybe I'd have a look at

Nathaniel Riley's butter and cream and try to strike up a conversation. Anyone who'd been in Broomewode a long time could offer a clue to my parentage.

I followed Susan to the stack of crates at the other end of the barn and explained that the order had swollen since I'd let the cat out of the bag about her tasty happy eggs. "Now Florence, Gaurav, *and* Hamish want a dozen each, too."

"Goodness," Susan said, sounding pleased. "I'll have to cut you a finder's fee. But the baking contestants might have to hang on a little longer. It's the hunt tomorrow, and the earl is hosting his famous post-hunt breakfast at the manor house for all his cronies. Katie Donegal is due to pick up a huge order of eggs."

My heart sank. So much for me thinking that Susan wouldn't run out. Argh. What if my friends suspected me of sabotaging their bakes?

"Don't look so worried, Poppy," Susan said. "The hens will lay plenty more by the morning. Oh, and the basil's particularly abundant. I picked you a bunch thinking you might like to make a strawberry and basil tart."

She handed me a bunch of the fragrant herbs, and I inhaled their distinctive scent. "Wonderful," I said, thanking her. "That's a great idea."

Susan was packing up the inn's eggs and honey when I heard a familiar Irish lilt. "And aren't you a sight for sore eyes."

I turned and there was Katie Donegal, beaming. Her curly gray hair had been trimmed, and her green eyes shone from her round, friendly face.

"Morning, luvvies," she said, greeting us both with a smile that was as warm as a hug. I didn't trust Broomewode's head cook as much as I once had. I was convinced she knew more about my mother, who'd been a helper in her kitchen, than she was letting on. I had no idea why she'd keep secrets about someone she hadn't seen in twenty-five years, but not only did she seem to have forgotten the existence of Valerie, but when the old gamekeeper, Mitty, started to talk about the past, she found ways to prevent him telling me anything useful. Of course, poor Mitty had suffered a stroke and wasn't as sharp as he probably had been.

The old cook threw up her hands. "On top of the eggs, I've come for all the raspberries you can spare, Susan."

Susan said she had quite a few punnets but had to hold some back for the weekend markets. "At this rate, Broomewode is going to eat me out of produce." She looked quite pleased.

I was glad for Susan. The more business for the farm, the better.

But Katie appeared not to hear. She was wringing her hands. "Lady Frome has had a last-minute change of mind, you see, and now she wants raspberry *and* lemon tarts for tomorrow's hunting breakfast. Her indecisiveness will be the death of me, I swear." Katie paused and fanned her pink cheeks with her hand. "In fact, this whole breakfast is turning into a palaver. I'm furious with the butcher—he overcharged me for the sausages and bacon knowing I'd never be able to get that much meat elsewhere in time."

"Oh, you and Derek are always at odds," Susan said, shaking her head. "If he's not overcharging you, the steak's too fatty or the sausages are too small."

"Small sausages are no laughing matter," Katie said, her face perfectly serious. "Derek is a swindler if ever I saw one. If it were up to me, I'd go a little farther afield for our meat, but the earl insists on Derek. Lord Frome is a man who respects tradition, and so do I, mind, but when a tradesman's a swindler, I say enough's enough."

Susan said, "The earl can't blame you at least if the sausages aren't up to par. Here are your berries." She handed Katie a few punnets full of bright and juicy fruits. "And your eggs are all crated up."

My eyes widened at the number of eggs headed for one breakfast. No wonder Susan didn't have enough to spare for the contestants. Those poor hens needed a nice long sleep before they'd even be able to think about laying some more. "Good. I'll send one of the lads to fetch them. But I'll be needing a few extra eggs if you can spare them, for Mitty. He's enjoying his egg every morning and getting stronger by the day."

"So Mitty is feeling better?" I said, trying to keep the hope out of my voice but failing miserably. I'd tried to talk to Mitty about the past. He'd been gamekeeper when my mother had worked at Broomewode. Would he remember her? And might he have noticed a man hanging around her who could be my father? It was so frustrating that she was looking after Mitty after his stroke and had all but thrown me out of the cottage before I could get any satisfactory information.

Katie looked at me sharply. "Yes, but he's not strong enough for another interrogation."

Maybe I'd been a bit eager, possibly a tad pushy, but interrogation was kind of harsh. Yeesh. Katie was furiously guarding Mitty from any outsiders. I tried not to take it personally.

I promised not to visit Mitty again until he felt stronger.

The last thing I wanted was to wear the poor man out. He'd been through enough.

Katie's face fell. "He might be physically stronger, but I think Mitty's marbles are getting away from him. He's obsessed with the past and talking nonsense. I wouldn't want anyone hearing him rant his crazy stories." She shook her head as Susan handed her the eggs for the retired gamekeeper.

Obsessed with the past? Ranting stories? Sounded like that was exactly what I wanted to hear. I'd give it a couple of days and then try again. There had to be some way to wheedle past Katie's protective shield. Maybe Mitty could be a new lead on my past after all.

Sly bounded into the barn and let out a happy bark. Katie bent to stroke him but straightened quickly, complaining of a bad back. "The earl and the countess have been working me to the bone, so they have. I'm not as sprightly as I was when I started there thirty-odd years ago. I'll be glad when this breakfast is over."

Susan said she had just the tonic and went to the shelves for one of her herbal remedies.

Sly barked again, a series of sweet but insistent woofs. "He needs walking," Susan called out, still ransacking her shelves. "I've neglected him this morning to get all the produce ready, and now he's got the energy of a pup."

I offered to throw his ball around outside before heading back to the inn and kissed both women goodbye on the cheeks.

Sly led the way out of the barn and rushed toward his red ball. I set down the heavy basket and obliged him with some of my best throws (admittedly, they didn't land too far away), and Sly woofed merrily. Susan's herb garden smelled incredible. There was something so vibrant and alive about that earthy, green smell. As Sly ran, I walked around the front of the farmhouse, exploring the rockery and its planted hedges. The lavender bushes were beginning to bloom, and their heady perfume mingled with the other green herbs. I had no idea how Susan managed to keep the garden so healthy and well-tended while looking after the farm. Maybe Reg lent a hand? If only I could stay here all morning, letting the sun soak into my skin, and indulge this lovely creature until my arm was too stiff. But no, I had cakes and tarts to make and a very important coffee date. It was time to get back to reality.

I gave Sly a firm pat on the haunches and said I'd see him later. "Look after your mom," I whispered into his furry ear. "She's a busy lady."

Sly barked in what I decided was the affirmative, so I picked up my weighty basket and made my way back to the inn.

As I walked, I couldn't stop my mind from whirring. I needed to find a way to convince Katie to let me visit with Mitty. Obviously, I didn't want to overexert him or impair his health, but if he was talking about the past anyway, why not give him a captive audience? I'd have to think of something clever to get into her cottage again. Maybe my meeting with Joanna would provide some answers and then Katie wouldn't be able to argue with the facts. I was getting a bit tired of her excuses. Katie was clearly keeping something from me.

I was so busy plotting and planning that I gasped when I rounded a bend and noticed Benedict coming toward me on the path.

"Poppy," he said warmly. "Keeping Susan's hens busy, I see."

Benedict was wearing a teal shirt that brought out hazel tones in his eyes. His brown hair was growing longer, curling slightly at the ears, and the effect was boyish. Perhaps even a little charming.

I wished him a good morning, and I asked what the day had in store.

"Edward and I are planning a route for tomorrow's fox hunt," he explained.

I rolled my eyes. "What is it with everyone and this cruel sport? How could you participate in something so barbaric?"

Benedict looked alarmed. "How could you think I'd kill for sport? We practice Trail Hunting. There's no actual fox." He rubbed his temple. I could tell my outburst had upset him, and I felt bad.

"I guess, well, I don't really understand," I confessed.

"Killing foxes for sport has long been banned in this country. But hunters still love the chase, as do our hounds. Think of Trail Hunting as a simulation of traditional hunting. We lay trails across our land with a scented cloth, which the hunters can follow on foot or on horse, and the hounds follow the scent. It's good fun for the whole family, and there's no bloodshed. Not cruel at all, unless you count my spending a day in ditches and across endless fields as cruel. We lay the scent through hedgerows and woods, along ditches, across fields, in order to simulate the natural movement of the wild fox. We never even see a fox—and if a hound does find one, we stop the hunt immediately and redirect it. It's all absolutely aboveboard."

As he spoke, Benedict's face softened and his eyes

glowed. I could see how much tradition meant to him, and I admired how he'd found a way to update this heritage to be kinder.

I nodded. "That does sound kind of beautiful. And the hounds don't mind chasing a pipe dream?"

Benedict laughed and rested his hand on my shoulder for a moment. "Don't worry. They love the excitement and the fuss and get a hearty meal at the end. Just like the humans. We're all simple creatures." He patted his stomach, although it appeared to be flat as a washboard.

I was about to ask more about the hunters' tastes when Edward, the new gamekeeper, came strolling up the path. He was wearing the green gamekeeper uniform and looked happier than I'd ever seen him. We said hello, and I told him that Benedict had been schooling me in the countryside ways.

"Exciting, isn't it?" Edward said. "I can't wait until the morning. Like a kid on Christmas Eve. The only person more excited is the earl," he added, turning to Benedict. "Your father insists that every detail be perfect. He's keen to follow every tradition."

"It's like Christmas and his birthday rolled into one," Benedict said. He sounded a little exasperated.

"You better make some extra cakes for the afternoon rush at the inn," Edward added. "It's like a party after the hunt. Those not lucky enough to be invited to the hunt breakfast at the hall will be packed round the inn. After a few hours in the outdoors, they'll have huge appetites."

Benedict replied, "You could join us if you like? Assimilate fully into Broomewode Village tradition."

There was a twinkle in his eyes. I couldn't tell if Benedict was teasing me or if the offer was genuine. Either way, I had to work tomorrow and said as much.

Out of nowhere, Benedict suggested that Edward take a look at a trail on the other side of the hill. Edward raised his brows but agreed with a small nod of his head. "See you later, Poppy. Don't forget to bake up a storm for tomorrow! And save me some of your lovely chocolate cake."

I promised him an extra big piece. Benedict didn't follow Edward, and we stood for a moment in silence. I couldn't think of a thing to say and told Benedict I should be getting back to the inn. I did have all those cakes to get started.

"Er, before you go," he said. "I was glad to bump into you just now."

I waited for him to continue, but no more words were coming out. I smiled encouragingly. Was he going to ask me to bake something extra for tomorrow's hunt? I really wasn't sure I had the time.

"I've been thinking," he said finally, "and well, I wondered whether you'd like to have dinner with me."

"Dinner?" I repeated, confused.

"Yes, you know, steak and chips or roast chicken. Vegetable tagine. Whatever you fancy."

"Dinner? Together?" I was so taken aback, I couldn't think of anything sensible to say.

"It's more entertaining than dining on one's own, don't you think?"

I swallowed. Was this really happening? Was Benedict asking me on a date? And why did it feel nice? Lovely, in fact. Oh, my goodness. Could it be that I actually had a crush on Benedict Champney?

Benedict laughed. "It's just dinner. I've been wanting to get to know you better."

I put a palm to my cheek. The skin was hot to the touch.

I *did* have a crush on Benedict Champney.

"That would be nice," I said slowly, still half amazed at my own feelings as they rose to the surface.

Benedict visibly breathed out. "Good," he said. "I had a little place in mind, far away from the prying eyes and keen ears of the village. Are you free tomorrow evening?"

I nodded, slightly embarrassed that I didn't have any plans for a Friday night.

"Well then," he said, stepping back. "That's settled. I'll message you the time and place."

There was a pause. Benedict stepped forward again, then swiftly bent down and kissed my flaming cheek. My heart raced. He smelled like vetiver and soft woods.

I waved goodbye, and we went in our separate directions, my head in a whirl and my pulse racing.

"Well, well," I said aloud. "Well, well."

CHAPTER 3

*M*y heart went back to its usual plodding beat the moment I returned to the kitchen and saw Gerry playing tricks on Ruta. I'd had a nice quiet morning sans spirit, but I'd been naïve to hope it would last. Poor Ruta. Every time she put her special Japanese knife down, Gerry moved it to the opposite side. She'd spin on the spot, bemused, before shaking her head and reaching for the knife once more.

He caught sight of me, and I made a slashing motion with my hand across my throat. Gerry flew to my side. "What are you saying, Pops? Cut it out?" He cracked up at his own joke.

I'd have loved to reply, but obviously it would only confuse Ruta more if I started talking to thin air. I put my basket onto the work table.

"Hey, Poppy," Ruta called out.

Luckily, Ruta was thoroughly immersed in chopping celery, so I took my time putting the farm produce in the larder and figuring out how to calm my racing mind. There was no way I could process what had happened with Benedict. The last woman I'd seen him with was an international celebrity doctor. Now he was asking *me* out? I was going to have to park it until later. For now, I had to take one thing at a time. Work came first and then, despite Susan's warning not to get my hopes up, I was super excited about my meeting with Joanna this afternoon. Maybe all my sleuthing about my past was going to finally pay off.

I returned to my workstation, and with Edward's words about hungry hunters echoing in my head, I set about making a double batch of carrot cake. Maybe I could go with Susan's suggestion about a strawberry and basil tart tomorrow. Probably I was showing off for the guests who didn't normally frequent the inn. I thought about it and decided I didn't mind showing off a bit if it meant more business. Besides, Ruta had a reputation as an innovator. I should try to keep up.

Gerry floated over, turning a somersault in the air.

"What ya got there? Carrots? You making the cream cheese frosting? Have you heard about the great hunt happening tomorrow? I feel sorry for the foxes, I do."

I felt sorry for him and irritated in equal measures. It's not like I could answer all those questions with Ruta and Pavel in the kitchen.

I widened my eyes as my way of communicating "can't talk right now." I'd have to explain about the foxes later. I didn't want anyone going around thinking Benedict was involved in a cruel sport. Not that I'd divulge any feelings about Benedict. Not to a bored, lonely ghost. Gerry floated about in my business enough already.

I weighed out the huge batches of flour, sugar, and butter and let my hands take over. Ruta had turned on the radio, and a nineties pop song came on. I couldn't remember the name of the singer, but the lyrics came to me instantly. I was shocked; I didn't have any memory of hearing the song before. But it was as if the words were hidden in some room of my memories. I just had to unlock the door. It was just like when I remembered the melody Katie Donegal was singing a few weeks back. Was this what Mitty was experiencing, too? Fragments of memories bursting into the present with no apparent connection to one another? And then a chilling thought struck me: Could I know more about my birth parents than I thought I did? Were there other snippets of memories buried so deep I hadn't yet unearthed them?

I shook my head like I was trying to get water out of my ears. The mind was a mystery but not one that I could solve. I got myself together and was about to pour my cake batter into tins when Gerry tumbled into me.

"Hey, Pops, I think you'd better add the grated carrot to that first?"

I blinked, confused, and then looked down at my chopping board. A huge mound of grated carrot looked back at me, mockingly. I put my palm to my forehead.

"Nice save," I whispered to Gerry. He could be a pain in the butt, but he was also my friend.

"You're welcome. You know I'm head of Team Poppy. I consider it my duty. Besides, the carrot in the carrot cake is important. Essential, one might say. You need to pay more attention to what you're doing."

I had to stifle a giggle. Since when did Gerry talk so much sense?

"Poppy," Ruta said, "Pavel and I are going to unload the delivery van. Hold the fort?"

"Sure thing," I replied. Holding the fort, or just holding it together, was something I was going to have to get better at. I scraped the carrot into the batter and mixed the lot together.

Gerry waited until we were alone and then perched himself on the edge of my worktop. "Something's up with you. What gives?"

I was shocked Gerry was so perceptive. He hadn't been like that in life, but no doubt now that he was an observer of people, he'd become sensitive. I had no interest in telling him a guy with a title had asked me out, so quickly I told him about my upcoming meeting with Joanna. "I'm so excited. She could really be the breakthrough I've been hoping for. Gerry, she actually knew my mother."

Gerry didn't look as thrilled for me as I'd hoped he would. There weren't many people I could talk to about my past, and he was someone I knew I could trust as he literally could not blab my secrets even if he wanted to. He said, "I wish I could go with you to meet this Joanna." He was limited to the inn and the competition tent where he'd died.

I poured the batter into the tins. "Really? Why?" Probably he just wanted to see some different scenery, but I was secretly glad not to have him as an invisible third person in a meeting that meant so much to me.

"I don't trust her, Pops."

I stopped pouring and looked at Gerry, confused. "Why? She's just a woman who grew up here. She worked at the hall the same summer my mother did. What on earth makes you say you don't trust her?"

"I don't know. Maybe it's because she comes from Broomewode. There's something about this place. You can't deny that it's peculiar." He folded himself into a pretzel shape and hung from the light fixture. Nothing peculiar about that!

"We're on an energy vortex here." I'd tried before to explain what I didn't fully understand myself. I was still pretty inexperienced as a witch, but there was definitely power here. "We're in line with Glastonbury, and you know how spiritual that is."

He snorted. "Couldn't throw a stone in Glasto without hitting a witch, a shaman or someone downright peculiar. Had a girlfriend once who went there on a goddess weekend. I am not joking. Came home and expected me to worship her, I swear."

I really didn't want to know about Gerry's past dating life. "Well, anyway, this energy vortex explains most of what seems a bit strange." I was probably trying to convince myself as well as him.

"I'm just saying, keep your wits about you. You won't have your guardian ghost with you."

Ruta and Pavel were returning with the meat delivery, so I promised to be careful. But as far as I was concerned, the remainder of my shift couldn't go fast enough.

AT THREE P.M. on the dot, I said goodbye to my co-workers and disappeared to the inn's glamorous bathrooms to freshen up. I'd brought a small vanity case with makeup and hair-brushes to make sure I looked my best. I wanted to impress Joanna—she was the closest person to my mother I'd yet come across. Maybe a part of me was thinking that if Joanna was impressed by me, then my mom would be, too. Wherever she was.

I stared at my reflection in the mirror—lips freshly glossed, a lick of mascara across my eyelashes, hair pulled back into a sleek, swinging ponytail. I'd added a small pair of gold hoops to my outfit and retied the bow of my shirt. I opened my bag. Inside my notebook, I'd tucked the picture of Valerie, the woman I believed was my mother, at the Broomewode Hall garden party. If Joanna's recollection of those days was foggy, maybe it would jog her memory. If I looked anything like my birth mom, then hopefully Joanna would spot a resemblance.

The drive to the next village filled my windshield with sumptuous views. Nothing but green hills and billowy trees, the air balmy and the sun golden. It was a day that felt like a blessing, a sanction from the sky gods that approved of my search for my birth mom. I had to stop myself from speeding along the country lanes. *Don't mess it up now, Pops. Some answers are finally within your grasp.*

I'd never visited Larkville before, so I followed my sat nav down a long, winding road that followed the lines of a steep grassy hill. Sheep grazed to my right, and on the left, a tractor toiled at the top of the hill. Behind the tractor, I glimpsed the bold, angular roof of a farmhouse, its charcoal slate glinting in the sun. I slowed my pace as up ahead, two fluffy sheep decided now was the time to cross the road. Luckily, there were no other cars around, so I hit the brakes and let what I could now see was a mama and her little lamb journey to the other field in their own time. Waiting (almost patiently), I lowered my window to let in a cool breeze. But the sound of shouting broke the charming scene. I swiveled in my seat and in the distance saw the outline of two men by the tractor. Their aggressive stance and wild gestures suggested some kind of argument was taking place. No doubt it was some farming dispute.

With a final bleat, the lamb made it across the road, and I headed off again, anxious to be on time for Joanna.

At the bottom of the hill, Larkville revealed herself to me. She was almost as beautiful as Broomewode, with matching cobbled streets, golden brickwork, and a small high street with a few independent shops. I spotted The Hourglass café on the corner immediately and parked outside. My heart was racing and my palms were sweaty. I needed to chill out, so I took a few deep breaths. *Time for answers.*

I pulled out the only photo I had of the woman I believed was my mother. I mustn't mess this up. Quickly I placed my hand on the photo. For me, magic was more instinctive than learned, as I was so new at my craft. Other than the ability to see certain ghosts—whether I wanted to or not—I'd never known I was a witch until a couple of months ago. It explained so much about why I'd always felt different, but since I hadn't grown up with the guidance of others like me, I was finding my way as though feeling ahead in the darkness.

Spirits of air, earth, water, and fire,
Let my eyes see and my ears hear
Whatever this woman has to say.
May I hear the message she would convey.
So I will, so mote it be.

I felt more focused and powerful for saying my made-up spell, and that gave me the confidence to enter the café.

A bell above the door dinged, and a woman sitting by the window looked up at me. A cold shiver crept down my spine, and my arms began to tingle. This was Joanna. I knew it, even though I also knew I'd never set eyes on her before. Weird. *Super* weird. Could it be that Joanna was a witch like me? Is that why I was feeling an instant bond? A sense of kinship? Argh. If only that was something you could ask a stranger: *Hi, nice to meet you. Are you a witch as well?*

The woman smiled and stood. "Poppy?"

I grinned and nodded. Here she was: Joanna, the woman who had known my mother during the summer she worked at Broomewode. I had the urge to throw my arms around her but checked myself before I fatally embarrassed both of us. All things considered, I was lucky Joanna had even accepted my invitation to talk. On the phone, I couldn't tell if she was being polite or actually really nice. Ever since I'd first come to Broomewode, my search for my parents had been like a series of outstretched hands gently guiding me and then slipping out of reach. It was so hard to tell, even now, with this smiling woman ahead of me, if someone was an ally or an enemy.

But then Joanna waved me over, and I felt another rush of warmth. She looked younger than forty-seven, with shiny blond hair cut into a thick, chin-length bob. Behind a pair of champagne-colored square glasses, warm brown eyes blinked at me, full of curiosity. And kindness, too. Could it be that she shared the same feeling of recognition?

She gestured for me to sit on one of the café's comfy brown leather chairs. On the square wooden table sat a carafe of water, two small glasses, and a steel cafetière of coffee. I noticed that Joanna had been reading a paperback, but the cover was folded back on itself.

"Was I late?" I asked in distress. Had I misunderstood the time? Great way to make a first impression.

"No. Not at all. I was early." She gestured to the cafetière. "I've ordered coffee, but they have tea, cold drinks. Whatever you like."

Her accent was neutral, hard to discern exactly where she was from.

"Black coffee's perfect," I said. "Thank you. It's been a long day."

"Has it been busy at Broomewode Inn?" Joanna pressed the plunger slowly and then poured two cups of steaming liquid. She passed the saucer to me, and I inhaled the earthy aroma. The café was busy, humming with people. The walls were white-painted brick and the floors polished wood. The tables were arranged around a red brick pillar, which took precedence in the center of the café. It was a lovely spot to meet, and I was thankful to be away from the village. I now understood why she chose a spot away from Broomewode. I didn't see anyone I knew. I could talk more freely here.

I nodded and told her how I wasn't naturally a morning person, so the early starts were a drag. She chuckled and said she was exactly the same. "The things I say to my alarm clock in the morning. I'm just glad it can't talk back!"

I was about to ask about her job when a petite waitress arrived at our table. She was wearing a quaint black pinafore with a ruffled neckline, and her brown hair was swept into a tidy bun at the nape of her neck. "Can I get you ladies anything to eat? We have a fine carrot cake on special today. It has a maple cream cheese frosting with toasted pecans."

I stifled a groan. Carrot cake? I'd iced enough of those this morning.

I thanked her but declined. I was too excited to have an appetite. Which was a first for me, that was for sure.

The waitress lingered, staring a little at Joanna. Was she working on cake commission or something?

"I'll take a slice of the special carrot cake," Joanna finally said, and the waitress nodded approvingly.

"Actually, I'm glad you ordered something," I said. "It's good for me to check out the local competition, but I couldn't stomach a whole slice."

"Happy to be of service," Joanna replied, "especially where cake is involved. I have a wicked sweet tooth. Which is why I'm so interested in hearing more about your job. How did you land the role at the inn? M-mother told me it's a widely coveted position."

Mavis would know that, as I bet she knew all the Broomewode gossip. My mind lingered on Joanna's choice of words —*wicked sweet tooth*. I always described my predilection for sweetness in the same way.

Joanna cleared her throat; I'd left her hanging. I flushed and regaled her with my story of the baking competition, my disastrous performance during bread week, and how I ended up replacing poor Eloise at the inn. Joanna was a good listener, and I would have lost track of time if the waitress hadn't returned with an enormous slice of cake.

"Well, the portions here are certainly larger than ours," I said, feeling my eyes widen. "I hope our customers don't think we're skimping. But I mean, who could eat all of this? It's half frosting."

"I'm not complaining. Maybe they baked too much and need to get rid of it," said Joanna.

I appreciated the reassurance. My gut reaction to Joanna

was that she was warm, friendly, and welcoming. While she tucked into a mouthful of cake, I took the opportunity to thank her for meeting with me. I knew it was a lengthy drive from Bristol, and she probably wanted to go straight to her mom's. I paused then, slightly ashamed of the white lie I'd told Joanna on the phone. It was much easier to evade the truth when a kind set of eyes wasn't looking straight at you. "You have no idea how hard it's been to find out anything about my cousin," I began. "All I have to go on is that he might have dated someone called Valerie. Sometimes it feels like the universe is conspiring against my search. You're my first real lead in weeks."

Joanna swallowed, and a flash of sadness crossed her face. "I'm so happy to meet you, Poppy, but I'm not sure I can be much help. It was so long ago, and I haven't seen Valerie in ages." She looked down at the plate. "Decades," she murmured.

"But your mother said you were in touch. That you used to meet up in the pub, go to concerts together. She even said you went to Glastonbury in a big group? Do you know who she was dating at the time? It could be my cousin."

Joanna smiled brightly. Too brightly. "Mum spends too much time at that paper. She thinks we're all as connected as she is to the community. The truth is, I've moved away. I have a busy life. I've lost contact with most of the people I used to know. Made new friends."

"And Valerie?" I asked, my heart in my throat.

"We lost contact when she moved to Glasgow. You might try going there."

"Glasgow?" My heart sank back down into my boots. That was miles away. What on earth had taken her that far north?

It was like she had purposely chosen somewhere as far from Broomewode Village as possible. But at least it was a firm lead. When the finals of the competition finished, maybe Hamish could help me track my mother. How far were the Highlands from Glasgow? I'd have to look it up later.

Joanna nodded, and it seemed like she wasn't going to say any more on the subject. But if she truly didn't know anything else, why agree to meet me? She could have said all that on the phone. I decided to press her for any memories she might have of the time when Valerie worked at Broomewode Hall.

"Can I ask why you are so interested in Valerie? This search is about your cousin, right?"

I bought some time by gulping down some coffee. It was still hot, and the liquid burned a little. Joanna waited patiently. I got the sense she was used to awkwardness. And I also got the sense that she knew I was lying. I looked down again and realized that the hairs on my arms were still standing on end. I felt sure there was some real connection between me and Joanna. I could trust her with the truth. And so I told her what I shared with very few people. "I believe Valerie was my mother."

Joanna's eyes widened behind her glasses. "Really? And your father?"

"I've no idea who my father was. I'm on a quest to discover where I really came from. Nothing is more important to me. I want to know where Valerie is and want to find out the identity of my birth dad, even though I'm pretty sure he's no longer around."

I took a deep breath and held it. There—I'd said it. I'd told a total stranger my deepest secret. So why did I feel so safe? Reassured even. Joanna was looking at me, a soft, diffuse expression on her face. I couldn't quite read it, but I also knew it was her way of saying, *Okay, go on. I'm listening.*

So I told her everything. All that I'd figured out so far. How I'd been left outside the Philpotts' bakery wrapped in a curious knitted blanket, which I still kept, as it was the only clue to my beginning. How I'd been watching *The Great British Baking Contest* and was convinced I'd seen my blanket, with its distinctive pattern, on the painting of the last Countess of Frome. She'd worn it as a shawl. I never would have tried out for a competitive baking show if I hadn't seen that as the best way to spend some time at Broomewode Hall.

Joanna listened, sipping her coffee. And when I stopped to refill my lungs, she smiled wistfully. "It's not much to go on, is it? A shawl that looks a bit like your baby blanket." I got the feeling she thought I was on the wildest of wild goose chases and felt my confidence dim. Then I pulled on the strength I'd felt in the car when I'd made up that spell. Even here, we'd be on part of the energy vortex I'd told Gerry about. This area attracted witches because of the mystic power, and I felt connected to others like me. I could draw on their power and intuition as well as my own.

I shook my head. "The pattern is the same. I've never seen it anywhere else. Please. Anything you can remember could help." I pulled out the photo of the garden party at Broomewode Hall and pushed it across the table.

"This is all I have of my mom. This, and the baby blanket she wrapped me in when she left me at the Philpotts' bakery. Do you remember anything about this party?"

Joanna slowly picked up the photograph and brought it closer to her face. She slipped her specs down her nose, and for the first time, I saw her brown eyes were flecked with gold.

She stroked the photograph, and then her finger trembled. What was she remembering? It was like I'd disappeared from the room, or in fact, more like the whole room had melted away. She seemed to be falling back in time. I waited, feeling the urgent charge of each second as it pulsed past. *Tick, tick, tick.* The seconds matched my heartbeat.

"That's the viscount." Her voice took on a dreamy quality. "It was his last summer, though none of us knew it at the time."

I nodded sadly. The viscount met a terrible ending, tumbling from a cliff while riding his beloved horse.

"And there's the countess. And dear Eileen."

I nodded again, getting impatient now. Did she recognize Valerie? I couldn't wait a moment longer and reached out, tapping at the photo with my pointing finger. "And that's Valerie..." I said, leaving it as a statement floating in the air.

"Yes," she said, "that's Valerie."

Phew. We got there. *Way to ramp up my blood pressure, Joanna.*

"Do you remember Valerie seeing anyone? Going on dates?"

Joanna still hadn't taken her eyes away from the photo. "She used to run off to London at the weekends. She was quiet about it, but everyone guessed she had a lover there. She was quite the scamp in those days. Always following her heart over her head."

I winced at the word lover. I mean, ewww, she was potentially talking about my dad. But at least it confirmed what Katie Donegal had told me, that Valerie was dating someone in the big city.

"Did she ever confide in you?" I asked hopefully. "Mention a name of who she was seeing in London? What he did? Where he lived?" I could hear the blood pounding in my ears. Was I about to discover the identity of my birth dad?

Joanna finally looked up. Her eyes had misted over. She pushed her glasses back up her nose and relaxed into her chair. It was like she had switched off the past. "Tom, I think his name was. He might have been a musician. I don't remember what instrument."

Argh. A musician? I'd seen the ghost of my father several times now, and there was not one thing about him that said musician. I mean, he was wearing robes most of the time. I sighed. In my bones, Joanna's new information didn't feel right. My dad didn't suit the name Tom. He was sooo not a musician. But why would Joanna lie? It didn't make sense. Maybe I should challenge her, push harder and see if she could have made a mistake? I was about to challenge her when Joanna screamed.

"What the?" I said and turned to follow Joanna's arm, which was pointing at the window. A tractor was racing straight toward us...and it was picking up pace!

CHAPTER 4

I leapt from my seat, sending coffee cups and plates flying. The table tipped over as I tried to scramble away from the window. I realized my legs were trapped beneath its heavy oak.

Everything blurred. Was time slowing down or speeding up? For a few terrifying seconds, I was free of gravity. My whole body seemed to lift and turn easily, moving swiftly with more speed and force than seemed possible. My breath caught in my throat. Joanna had leapt over the table, and suddenly I was on the floor, her body shielding mine.

Screams. A piercing cry. Then glasses shattering, crystalline, and a thunderous, roaring noise. Darkness. My eyes were squeezed shut. My body tingled. Waves and waves of electricity. What. Was. Happening?

And then a calamitous crash. Deafening. Steel squealing and a great thud.

I could barely breathe beneath the weight of Joanna's body. My nose filled with the scent of coconut shampoo.

DID I lose consciousness for a second? My head ached and ached. Something warm trickled at my temples. I realized my eyes were shut, and I opened them, slowly, just letting in the light.

I wasn't prepared for the sight that greeted me. A yellow tractor had collided with the brick pillar in the center of the coffee shop. People had scattered—crouched beneath tables, pressed against walls. A sudden ringing in my ears. A clothy, weighted silence, and then more screaming.

I wriggled beneath Joanna, trying to break free. She felt my movement and peeled herself off my squished body. I took deep gulps of air. My head throbbed; my ribs throbbed. Joanna extended a hand, and I grasped it, letting her pull me to my feet. Upright, the scene was even more chaotic. People were crying, porcelain plates and cups and saucers scattered across the wooden floors. Shimmering pools of fractured glass, spilled coffee and tea. Cakes crushed underfoot. I stared at the tractor. It was empty. No one in the driving seat. But then how did it crash into the shop? Nothing made sense. But my immediate concern was Joanna. Blood dripped from her forehead; the wound looked deep.

"Are you okay?" she asked me worriedly. "There's some blood on your neck. I think you caught the side of the table."

"I think you saved my life," I whispered, shaking my head. "That was quite the ninja move." Everything was so surreal. I touched my neck. It was warm and sticky. When I pulled my fingers away, they were red, but there was no wound. "It's your blood," I said. "There's a deep gash on your forehead. You're really bleeding."

"Must have been a piece of flying glass." She lifted her right arm, and I saw it was bleeding too. "Here, too. But it's superficial." She glanced around at where we'd been sitting. If she hadn't pulled me out of the way, I'd have been killed. "Could have been so much worse," she said, and I shuddered.

She looked down at her arm and said, "I'll see if I can find some napkins." Before she could do that, our waitress began shouting, "Everyone out! Everyone out! It's hit the pillar. The roof is compromised."

More screams. I looked at Joanna in horror and then turned to the waitress. "We need to call 999."

"It's done. The police and an ambulance are on their way. Let's get out of here sharpish."

I glanced up at the roof. I hadn't been able to use my magic to stop the tractor—there hadn't been time—but maybe I could prevent the roof from collapsing until everyone was out.

I was too rattled to come up with a clever spell; I only stared at the roof and willed it to remain in place. Joanna grabbed my hand, and I felt the warm connection. I glanced at her and saw her head tipped back. She was staring up, and her lips were moving. Once more I wondered if she was a sister and doubled my concentration on the roof.

We were interrupted when the server handed Joanna a dish towel. "Here. It's clean. Press it on your forehead to stop the bleeding." I wondered if she was training to be a doctor or paramedic and worked part-time in the café to pay the bills. She was that calm and resourceful. Joanna thanked her and pressed the cloth to her bleeding head. Then she pulled me along, and we joined the throng of panicked people as they rushed out of the café. We gathered as one shivering, shocked group on the grassy lawn, bruised and cut, but thankfully no one appeared to be seriously injured. It was a miracle. I was still stunned and stared at the gap where the window had been, where Joanna and I had been sitting and chatting peaceably just a few minutes ago. What had caused the tractor to careen into the shop?

Joanna stepped into my view. Her face was creased with concern, cheeks streaked with blood and small cuts. I realized she wasn't wearing her glasses—they must have been knocked off when she leapt across the table. "Poppy, it's not safe here. You must leave."

"I know. That's why we've come outside."

Joanna shook her head. "That's not what I mean. Please. Listen to me..." She paused and looked beyond me, and I turned to follow her gaze. Two horses were galloping down the hill toward us. I squinted, trying to make out the shape of the silhouettes against the sun. I stepped forward. Could it be? Surely not. But yes, it was Benedict and Edward, galloping on two magnificent chestnut horses. They came toward the café at full gallop, the horses panting and snorting. I couldn't take my eyes off the sight, and then, when Benedict was close enough to lock eyes with mine, I saw the fear pulse in his face. "Whoaaa," he yelled and pulled on the reins. He jumped down with all the confidence of an expert rider. I stepped toward him as he rushed over.

"Poppy. Are you all right?" His eyes widened as he looked at me. Concern, clear as day, made its way into his features. For a moment, the tension in my body softened. He *cared*. "We heard the crash, but it was too late. Couldn't stop it." He held onto my hands as though needing to reassure himself I was truly alive. "Are you cut? Did you hit your head?"

I reassured Benedict I was fine, pointing at the window where the yellow tractor looked wildly out of place against the brick pillar in the middle of the café. "Though I was sitting right in its path."

"I can't believe it," he said and then turned back to me. "We need to get you seen to. Where's the ambulance? I want you checked over to be sure you're all right."

But my few bruises were the last thing on my mind. "I don't understand how it happened," I said. "Did you see anything from up there?"

Benedict shook his head. "No, Edward and I were marking the course for the hunt when we heard a tremendous crash."

I looked over at Edward, who was talking to the waitress as though he knew her.

Behind Benedict, another man came running down the hill. He was red in the face and out of breath, his chest heaving. From the look of his overalls and the smear of mud on his forehead, he was the village farmer.

"What happened?" he cried, clearly upset.

Benedict glared at him. "Your tractor nearly killed a load of innocent people." I'd never heard him sound so coldly furious. He was every inch the lord.

The farmer looked incredulous. He stepped forward and peered through the window. The other café customers picked up where Benedict left off. Cries of "You should be more careful" and "I could have been killed" and "Just look at this cut on my arm" reared up and carried over the breeze. The farmer's color deepened. He raised his palms in front of him, as if asking for mercy. "The brakes must have failed, and the tractor rolled down the hill itself. There's no other explanation. I'd parked it for the day. It was empty."

In the distance, the sounds of sirens grew louder. The ambulance must be arriving. I didn't need medical help, but Joanna certainly did. I spun around to make certain she was looked at, but Joanna was no longer by my side.

"Where is she?" I said to Benedict.

"Who?"

"Joanna. The woman I was standing with a moment ago. She's got a nasty wound on her head and a deep gash on her arm." The ambulance pulled up outside the café, and two paramedics leapt out of the front. The sight of their smart uniforms was reassuring. I watched as they assessed the scene and began to triage patients, prioritizing head wounds. Which was exactly what Joanna had. What if she was concussed?

"I didn't see anyone," Benedict said.

"She was right here."

"I promise you, Poppy, you were standing all alone when I spotted you. You looked completely dazed. You gave me the shock of my life."

Could that be true? He was talking as though Joanna didn't exist at all. I clapped a hand to my chest. Was Joanna a ghost? Had I somehow missed the signs? I closed my eyes. Did the outline of her body flicker like the other spirits I'd encountered? No, definitely not. And I was pretty sure ghosts couldn't email or communicate by telephone. Also, I'd never known a ghost who could drink coffee and knock me down. But what if she was some other, more evolved spirit? A kind I'd never seen before? There was still a lot I didn't know about the spirit world.

I opened my eyes again.

"Poppy, you seem really shaken up," Benedict said softly. He took my hand and squeezed it. "Let's get you over to the paramedics."

I shook my head. "Really, I'm fine." But I wondered. Had the fall knocked the sense out of me? Surely Joanna wasn't a ghost. Maybe she'd just wandered off. To her car maybe? She must be somewhere.

"I need to find Joanna," I told Benedict. "She's the one who's hurt. She must be here somewhere." Could she have walked away and fainted? She'd saved my life. I had to find her.

I tried to close my ears to Benedict calling me to come back. I searched the crowd of customers and workers who were huddled together, shocked and confused. I searched and searched for a flash of Joanna. Nothing.

Panic rose in my chest, and I felt short of breath. I walked the circumference of the café, calling her name. Nothing.

I kept walking, desperation mounting. It didn't make sense; she was right beside me just a moment ago. The scene was still chaos. People were shocked, as well they should be —they'd brushed closer with death than most. But in the scattered, milling crowd, there was still no sign of Joanna. It was like she'd slipped into thin air, spirited far from this place. I couldn't understand why she would do that—we'd just got to the heart of her memories. And she was wounded. She needed medical attention. I stopped circling, slowed to a feeling of motionless dread.

I took out my phone and dialed her mobile number. It went to voicemail. I felt sick. Was she okay?

Around me, people were getting into their cars and

driving away. I looked down the road, where several vehicles had already left the scene. It made perfect sense to want to get away from the site of the accident, but I approached strangers anyway, describing Joanna and asking if they'd seen her leave. Person after person shook their heads at me, apologized for not being able to help. Desperately, I peered into the backs of their cars like a crazy woman, as if they were hiding Joanna. But no. Nothing. She was gone.

The helpful server was now assisting the paramedics. I pushed my way forward and asked if she'd seen Joanna, the woman she'd given the tea towel to for her bleeding head. She looked up at me and said quite curtly, "No. But she should be seen to. That cut looked quite serious."

I agreed, but I could hardly get Joanna to the ambulance when I couldn't find her.

A woman who was sitting having her wrist bandaged looked up. "I saw a blond-haired woman holding a towel to her head drive off a few minutes ago. Thought she should have had stitches myself, but she got in her car and drove off." She nodded her head as though I might have argued with her. "She's gone."

CHAPTER 5

*J*couldn't figure it out. Why no goodbye? Why leave with a bloody arm and head and not even say goodbye? It didn't make sense. Nothing was adding up. Why did this always happen to me? It was like danger followed me wherever I went, including all the way to Larkville. But there was one thing I did know. Joanna had saved my life. And then she'd given me that strange warning right before she disappeared. She'd told me to leave, but why? And had she meant Larkville? Or was she telling me to leave Broomewode? I'd have loved to ask her, but she hadn't stuck around long enough.

Benedict was helping organize the shocked group remaining outside the ruined café, but he still found time to check in with me. "Did you find your friend?"

I felt bereft. "No. She left. I don't know why she'd leave. She was bleeding. Could she have been in shock? What if she gets in an accident?"

Benedict's concern turned to stubbornness. "I promise that we'll get to the bottom of it as soon as you've been checked out by the paramedics. Maybe you don't feel it because you're in shock, but you could be hurt. You were in the path of that tractor. You might have been hurt getting out of its way."

I looked down at my new pink shirt. It was ruined. Argh. As much as I hated to admit it, perhaps Benedict was right. In all the fuss, I'd forgotten that I'd hit my head on the side of the table. "I'd thought the blood was all Joanna's, but some of it was mine. It's just a flesh wound," I said. "Looks worse than it is. I'm fine."

"Let's let the experts decide." He smiled at me softly. "We need to protect all the brains you've got..."

Despite myself, I laughed.

He led me over to one of the paramedics, a young-looking man with a comfortingly no-nonsense manner. He checked me over, flashing light into my eyes, asking me a series of questions, and when he felt certain I wasn't at risk of suddenly dropping dead, cleaned my cut and put a bandage on the wound. I thanked the man, who nodded and turned to his next patient.

"See, I told you," I said to Benedict, "fixed with a Band-Aid."

"Better safe than sorry. Why don't I drive you home?" Benedict offered. "I'm sure I can figure out how to drive that old Renault of yours," he said with a slight grin.

I shook my head. "It looks like you're needed here. Besides, you've got your horse to worry about. It's a kind offer but—"

Benedict jumped in. "Edward can sort that out."

"Let me drive myself home. I'll go slowly, I promise."

I could tell Benedict was exasperated with me, but I was

as stubborn and single-minded as he was. He asked me to text him as soon as I got back to my cottage, and I agreed. He embraced me, quickly but warmly, in an enveloping hug and then whispered, "Be careful, Poppy. I need you to stick around."

Despite everything, I glowed at his words.

"I promise."

I got into my car and pulled out my phone again. I tried Joanna's cell. Still nothing. I rattled off a quick email to her work address—subject line only—which read, *Where did you go? Are you OK?* and then turned the key in the ignition. I had every intention of keeping my promise, but I knew I couldn't go back to the cottage yet. I needed to check if Joanna had left to visit her mother's house, as was her original plan. Maybe the accident fueled her desire to see her mom and she'd simply left in a panic. I'd drive through Broomewode Village first, pick up Gateau, and then —home.

I made my way out of the car park, joining the line of cars waiting to turn back onto the road.

As I drove back toward Broomewode, shaken and trying to process what had just happened, I felt my gaze drawn to the hills. There was a hawk, circling. My hawk, I was almost certain, and on the hill, a lone rider heading in the same direction as me. I suspected I had two protectors watching over me. The hawk, and I was certain that was Benedict riding along the ridge.

Perhaps it was over-the-top of Benedict to act like a hero on horseback, but still I felt comforted. In this crazy world I found myself in, I wasn't alone.

The hawk's long wingspan was silhouetted against the

late afternoon sun. The hawk. Had he been in Larkville this whole time but I was too distracted to notice?

As I carefully followed the road back to Broomewode, I wondered why the hawk was following me now that the danger had passed. Or was he still here because the danger hadn't disappeared? What if the tractor crashing into the coffee shop was no accident? A chill ran over me. I mean, firstly, why would a stationary tractor with no driver just take off like that? I'd overheard the farmer saying in a loud voice that the brakes must have been faulty, but why fail at that exact moment? What could have possibly caused them to burn out so suddenly if nothing had been wrong before? And why had the tractor crashed through the exact window where I was sitting?

Above me, the hawk let out an almighty screech. I couldn't help but feel it was a warning. And then I remembered Joanna's last words to me. *It's not safe here. You must leave.* I'd assumed Joanna was worried about the building collapsing, but maybe that wasn't what she meant at all. Here was yet another person telling me to leave Broomewode. Someone I barely knew telling me I was in danger. That it wasn't safe in the village. Why were so many people determined to get rid of me?

Joanna completely puzzled me. I'd felt like I knew her. The contact we made was real. Could it be that Joanna was a witch? She was born in Broomewode, after all. Was that why I recognized her instantly? Was it a coven sister thing? But it wasn't the same as with Elspeth, Eve, and Susan. It was more *comfortable*, somehow. Then she'd risked her life to save mine and mysteriously disappeared without saying goodbye.

I had so many questions and no idea how to answer a single one.

I wound down my window, let the fresh air breeze in, cooling my temples, which were still throbbing. I was desperate for clarity, to understand how that tractor had seemingly made its own way down the hill, but nothing was adding up. The suspicion that the incident was, in fact, a treacherous, sneaky attempt on my life was growing by the second. It had horrible echoes of the day I was picking wild gooseberries on the outskirts of Susan's farm with Sly and Gateau. I could recall the scene so vividly. The old tower was made of the same golden stone as the farm and Broomewode Hall, with a luscious crop of vivid gooseberries at its base. I'd never had the pleasure of foraging for gooseberries before, and I remember thinking how beautiful they were when Sly and Gateau went berserk and there was a sudden rumbling and a huge slab of stone fell from the top of the tower. There was an enormous crash as stone hit stone, and small pebbles bounced. It landed exactly where I'd been standing before Sly scooted me out of the way just in time. Just like Joanna did. Just in time.

But if the tractor accident was some kind of planned attack, how would anyone even know that I was at The Hourglass coffee shop? The only person I'd told was Susan, my ally and sister witch.

I turned the corner, and Broomewode Village came into view, its magnificent rolling hills behind and to the side of me and the picturesque high street ahead. The rows of cottages had bountiful hanging baskets, bright colors erupting at all angles, the petals soft and curving away from their leaves. What evil was lurking behind all this beauty?

If the attack wasn't an accident, I couldn't believe Susan was behind it, but could she have told someone I was going to be there?

I dragged in a sharp breath as I remembered Katie Donegal—she'd come into Susan's produce barn just as I was leaving. Was it possible she'd heard me tell Susan where I was going that afternoon? I had no clue how long she'd been standing there before she announced herself. I shook my head. What exactly was I accusing Katie of? Yes, it was true that she was acting very suspiciously about Mitty—not wanting to let him talk about the past. But I'd chalked that up to an overprotective gene. Nothing more sinister than that. Could she have told anyone else where I was going? I couldn't think of a single good reason why she would. Hmm. Maybe I was heading down the wrong line of inquiry.

Who else had I seen today? Benedict, of course, and Edward, too. But I was sure I hadn't told either of them my plans for the afternoon. No, I was far too busy berating them both about fox hunting...and then being schooled about how wrong I was, of course. (How I hated being wrong.) But I was certain that Benedict, Edward, and Susan were on Team Poppy. I mean, I didn't even want to consider the possibility that wasn't the case. Maybe it was more likely that my imagination was in overdrive. Probably the runaway tractor was an unfortunate accident, as the farmer suggested.

But then why had Joanna warned me to leave?

Another, equally horrible suspicion crossed my mind. What if it wasn't me the tractor was meant to kill after all?

What if it was Joanna?

My mission now was to find Joanna. I'd head straight to the newspaper office to find Joanna's mom. With the disaster at Larkville, the paper would be busy, and that was surely the most likely place she'd be. Maybe Joanna had popped in to give her eyewitness account.

IF I HAD any expectations of slipping into the inn's bathrooms to freshen up unnoticed, then I was sorely misguided. Eve was at the back entrance by the parking lot, Gateau at her feet. She was sitting on the stone step and leapt to her feet when she saw me.

"Dearie, there you are. My senses have been trembling for the last hour. Something happened to you—but what is it?"

She rushed closer, and then her eyes grew wide with alarm. "You're bleeding! I knew it. My instincts are never wrong. Tell me you're okay?"

I'd hit my head and had a cut on my jaw, but I didn't feel too bad. Eve came closer and studied me. "I'm fine," I whispered. She smelled of cinnamon, and her presence was comforting. Suddenly the adrenaline that had been coursing through my body flowed out again. I was exhausted. Tired to the very bone. Shaken up and shocked.

Gateau mewed violently at my heels, nudging my ankles with her nose, demanding attention.

Eve drew back and looked at me. "She went wild about thirty minutes ago. Raced into the pub, making circles around the tables, meowing her head off."

I bent down, and Gateau jumped into my arms. She wriggled her way up and pushed her tiny, sweet face into mine. "I'm sorry," I told her. "I should have brought you with me. I stopped you doing your job." She meowed loudly. It sounded simultaneously like *So pleased to see you alive* and *How dare you leave me! You had no right!*

Eve was waiting patiently for me to explain what on earth had happened. I quickly filled her in about my meeting at The Hourglass coffee shop and then the horror of a wayward tractor—heading full speed straight for me.

As I spoke, Eve listened carefully. I could tell she was trying to piece together what happened but was puzzled too.

"My senses started twitching right about the time the tractor would have been rolling down that hill."

"Do you think that means it wasn't an accident?" I asked nervously, stroking the spot between Gateau's eyes.

Eve shrugged. "I wish I could say one way or the other, but it's impossible to tell. If we witches are deeply attuned to one another, any kind of threat will raise the alarm bells— accident or deliberate."

I sighed. I'd been hoping Eve could provide some clarification, but it wasn't going to be that simple.

"Let's get you inside, dearie, and clean up that wound. That paramedic did his best, but I have a healing balm with me that will seal up that wound in no time. Don't want a scar on that pretty skin."

I allowed Eve to usher me down to the small cellar room where staff could sometimes sleep if they were on back-to-back shifts. Inside was a single cot, neatly made up with stiff-looking white sheets, a basin with a mirrored medicine cabinet above it, and a copper rail for hanging clothes and uniforms.

"I can't stay long," I murmured as Eve cleaned my cut with a cool washcloth. As nice as it was to be looked after, I needed to find Joanna.

Once my cut was clean, Eve rubbed some kind of herbal-scented yellow balm onto the skin. I hissed a little at the sting, but Eve said the burn was a good sign—it was doing its job.

"I know you're going to tell me off," I began, but Eve cut me off.

"Yes, but I understand. It's your family. But this time, can you take that mog of yours? If anything dangerous is coming your way, she'll be on it in a flash. Gateau is an excellent familiar."

I grinned, a proud cat-mom, and agreed.

WITH GATEAU in the passenger seat, I was soon back in my Renault and heading for the newspaper office. I never usually drove in the village, preferring to walk, but I'd lost enough time tending to wounds, and I couldn't let Joanna slip away.

I pulled up outside *Broomewode News's* plain front, told Gateau to be on high alert, and then walked through the repurposed cottage door to see if Mavis was in. At the desk, the same bored woman was sitting staring into space as the last time I was here.

"Can I help you?" she asked, not sounding interested in helping anyone. "I must warn you, no one's here. Trim, the paper's only reporter and photographer, is off on assignment." She sounded very important. I knew exactly where Trim had gone and hoped he wouldn't find out I'd been there, as I did not want to be interviewed about my horrendous near-death experience. I asked if she could give me Mavis's address.

"Not allowed. Sorry."

"Trim will vouch for me," I said, determined to get what I needed from this woman.

"He's out at the scene of an accident, I'm afraid," the woman replied. She shifted in her chair.

No doubt we'd passed each other on the road? "With the tractor?" I asked.

The woman nodded. "How did you know?"

I swallowed. Being an eyewitness for the local paper was not something I needed right now. A white lie was in order. "They're talking about it at the inn."

The woman nodded, uninterested. Hmm. I was going to have to find a way to turn this disinterest into something positive. Maybe she'd be willing to give me Mavis's home address if it was less exhausting than having me stand here bothering her.

"I'm a friend of Mavis's daughter, Joanna, and she asked me to deliver something for her."

I could feel the color rising in my cheeks. I was a terrible liar, and I knew it. My dad always said I had zero poker face. It was something he was proud of—that he'd raised an honest daughter. But in the name of getting to the truth, a little lie could be forgiven, I was sure.

"Well, if it's actually Mavis you're after, why didn't you say? She's upstairs in her office." She shook her head at me like I was an idiot.

I felt my jaw drop open. "She's here?"

A flicker of annoyance crossed the woman's face. "Yes, I mean, she does work here, after all. You're welcome to go on up." She gestured to the staircase and then swiveled her chair away from me and back to an open magazine on a shelf below the desk. I glanced at the article headline: *Best Picnic Recipes For Lazy Summer Days.*

I climbed the staircase with mounting trepidation. Why was Mavis here instead of at home, waiting for her daughter's visit? Had she forgotten? Surely not. Joanna very explicitly said she wanted to meet at four p.m. so that she wouldn't be late for tea with her mom.

I knocked on the door to Mavis's office and waited a few beats before she called, "Trim? You back already?"

I opened the door and peered in. The smell of dust and aging newspaper hit me, but it was more nostalgic than unpleasant. Mavis was sitting at her old schoolteacher's desk, neat piles of papers stacked to her right, an old computer on a side table to her left. The blinds were pulled down low to block out the sun, and dust motes danced in the air.

Mavis looked up and was clearly surprised to see me. She was wearing a cream linen smock, which brought out the warmth in her deep-set brown eyes. "Oh, hello. I remember you. The young woman trying to find a long-lost relative."

"Wow. You have a good memory."

As though to prove my point, she said, "Poppy, isn't it?"

I smiled and nodded, apologizing for the sudden intrusion.

"No apologies necessary," she said. "I'm happy to have the company until Trim gets back." She leaned forward. "Did you hear about the disaster in Larkville?"

I nodded. It was true. I had heard. I'd also been there, which I'd keep to myself, though no doubt Joanna would tell her mother everything. I glanced around, but there was no sign my erstwhile coffee date had turned up here.

"Trim's excited to be first on the scene. It's not often our little local newspaper can compete with the big boys." She sounded pretty thrilled, too. "It's very good for us. As long as there's no fatalities, of course," she quickly added.

I stepped into the office, and Mavis told me to take a seat, which I would have done if every chair hadn't been covered with papers.

"Just move any pile you like, pet. I'm working my way through some old files. How's your search for your"—she paused—"cousin, was it? Coming along?"

I swallowed, remembering how I hadn't fooled her about searching for a distant cousin. She'd seen straight through me and knew it was for my birth dad. "Well, it's about that," I said. "I was wondering if Joanna was with you? I thought you were meeting her at your cottage, for tea, you see."

Mavis looked baffled. "Sorry, luvvie. I've no idea what you're talking about. Joanna?"

Now I was the one to be baffled. "Your daughter, Joanna. Remember how you gave me your daughter's email address and phone number last week because she went to school with Valerie?"

"Yes, of course, pet, but I don't see what that's got to do with Joanna coming here. We had no plans to meet today."

I blinked hard. Joanna had lied to me. She'd never intended to visit her mother at all.

Okay, of all the puzzles I was trying to work out, it wasn't the most cryptic, but why would she lie about visiting her mom?

More important, what else was she lying about?

CHAPTER 6

*B*ack in my cottage, I was so bewildered I told Mildred, my kitchen ghost, the whole story. She immediately began fussing over the small cut I'd received.

"You be careful, miss. A cut like that can turn nasty. Why, we lost the second undergardener at my last job. Nicked his thumb digging up potatoes, he did, and next thing I knew they were laying him out for burial."

I groaned. Mildred was still stuck in the Victorian era and really did not get that a cut wouldn't necessarily lead to septicemia and sudden death. I assured her I was fine, that what I really needed was a bit of peace and quiet. She floated out of the room in a great huff. Great. Today I'd narrowly missed death, been given the slip by my strongest lead, and now I'd offended a ghost. Mildred wasn't exactly a kindred spirit, but she was company, and I was definitely feeling a little bruised and in need of a sympathetic ear.

Gateau sensed my mood and leapt from the stone floor to the walnut table in one great jump. She sashayed over to face me, nudged my hand with her wet pink nose and then sat back on her haunches and cocked her head. *So, what now?* she seemed to be saying.

"What now, indeed," I replied to her little face.

To say I was feeling despondent was the understatement of the year. I felt like Death was trying to chase me from the village and no one was who they first appeared to be. My head was still aching from where Joanna body-slammed me to safety, so I decided to do as the Brits do and make tea. Not just any tea, though. Earlier in the week, Susan had loaded me up with a stack of her favorite dried herbs, and I combined a batch of her nettles with some soothing chamomile.

Watching the water boil, I tried to make sense of all that happened today and figure out what needed to be my priority. When I was a high school freshman and feeling overwhelmed by schoolwork, my adoptive mom taught me to mind-map what needed to be done and then arrange my points in order of importance. In later life, it was a method I'd used to get through the baking competition and then my huge stack of chores at the inn. I decided to apply it to what happened with Joanna.

I grabbed an old sketching pad and made a note of everything I noticed about Joanna and what we had talked about at The Hourglass before we'd been interrupted by a demon tractor. The blond hair, the square glasses, the warm smile, the tingling, buzzing sensation I'd felt when I first saw her, the way she evaded my questions, how I'd discovered that Valerie had moved from Broomewode to Glasgow, and finally how she'd reacted when I showed her the photo of the summer party, her comment about it being the viscount's last, the wistful expression, the soft way she'd touched the faces.

And then—my stomach dropped. The photo! I never got it back! Joanna had been holding my precious picture when the tractor came careening into the shop. After that, it was all a blur. Had she dropped the photo? Put it in her pocket? My mood dropped even lower. That photograph was the only image I had of my birth mom, and now I didn't even know where it was. I put my head in my hands. I was close to tears. Gateau scuttled closer and licked my fingers.

Where *was* Joanna? Why had she lied about meeting her mother in Broomewode today? And more importantly, was she okay? Her injuries weren't life-threatening, but they needed tending, and yet, instead of waiting for the paramedics, she'd disappeared.

"Where would someone go who had a bleeding head wound?" I asked Gateau, who just stared at me as though I might have a head wound.

"Of course," I said to Gateau, raising my head. "You're right. I'm being foolish. I'll try the local hospital. Maybe she went straight there."

Gateau mewed in what I figured was approval, so after making my tea and adding some of Susan's honey for extra fortification, I whipped out my phone, searched for the number and hit dial.

"Hi," I said when a man answered the hospital's main line. "I'm calling to see if a friend has been admitted to your hospital after a tractor accident. I was with her when it happened, but she disappeared shortly after."

There was a silence at the other end of the line and then, "Name, please? Yours and theirs?"

"I'm Poppy Wilkinson. I'm looking for Joanna..." Oh, no. What was Joanna's last name again? I closed my eyes and imagined Joanna's business card. "Crane," I said. "Joanna Crane. She might have been admitted a few hours ago."

"Hold the line, please."

Classical music, something string-based, tinkled down the line. Gateau jumped from the table into my lap, circled a couple of times, then snuggled in. I stroked the top of her head.

The phone clicked, and the music disappeared. "No one of that name has been admitted to this hospital in the last twenty-four hours."

My heart sank. I thanked the man and hung up.

"Now what?" I asked Gateau. She raised her head and then lowered it again as if to say, *I'm a familiar, not a miracle maker.* The hospital had been a long shot, but it was my last. Where was Joanna?

I tried her cell one more time. Nothing.

I figured there was nothing else I could do right now so decided to run myself a hot bath. I had some of my best ideas while soaking in the tub. I was a water witch, after all. Besides, a good soak with some special herbs would soothe my aching muscles and bruises. If Joanna wasn't lying about everything, then Valerie had moved to Glasgow, and I needed to know if she was still there.

I gently set Gateau down and went to the horseshoe-shaped bathroom. After the kitchen, it was my second favorite room in the cottage. I'd painstakingly tiled the floor myself in a shade of gray just lighter than the flagstone in the rest of the cottage. The walls were a complementary taupe, and a small, curtained window looked out over my back garden. But the *pièce de résistance* was undoubtedly the bath-tub. My dad had accompanied me as I trawled scrapyards for the perfect copper freestanding tub. We'd found a bargain Georgian tub and spent hours restoring the enamel together before one of his old friends came to help with the plumbing. The tub was deep and long, and when it was full, I felt cocooned in its warmth. We'd also found some antique marble on our travels, and he'd turned it into a platform for a square enamel sink with enough space left over to house my vanity case and a small gold mirror. It was my idea of perfection, and I thanked my lucky stars every time I got into its depths and soaked my weary body.

I turned the taps, and water gushed from the faucet. It took a while to fill, so I went to feed Gateau like the good cat mom I was.

By the time I returned, the room had steamed, and I tipped a good measure of my special mixture of salts into the tub. There were Epsom salts to soothe the aches, lavender to help me relax, geranium and rose for their scents alone, and a touch of sandalwood, among other things.

Before I sank into the scented water, I decided to try to summon my mother. Who better to give me an idea of what to do next? I'd call for her rather than wait passively for her to show up, as she'd done a few times before in visions. My powers were getting stronger by the week—I could extinguish flames on candles, and I'd been practicing turning locks on doors, so surely I could will a vision that had appeared out of nowhere in the past.

I sat on the edge of the tub and closed my eyes. If there was one thing I'd learned from Eve and Elspeth, it was that a little rhyming spell went a long way. I believed it was about focus, as I really had to concentrate to find the right words so there was no room in my head for distractions. Would I be powerful enough on my own to summon my mother? There was only thing I could do and that was to try my hardest. I needed answers. Fast.

I focused my mind on every image I had of my mother. The shadowy silhouettes, the outline of a pregnant belly, the soft voice, and the photo of her at the garden party, laughing, frozen in time by the camera, mouth open and eyes crinkled. She was tall and slight, wearing a high-waisted patterned skirt and a pink halter neck top. In her ears hung delicate drop earrings, though I'd never been able to figure out the stone.

As I concentrated, eyes squeezed shut, words began to appear in the darkness.

Earth below, Sky above,
Bring my mother full of love.
Let me see her with my eyes.
I seek the truth, scorn the lies.
Over the lands, the skies, and seas,
Bring my mother back to me.
So I will, so mote it be.

I repeated the spell three times, trying to feel the force of my coven sisters as if they were beside me. Sure enough, when I opened my eyes, the room felt different. It had grown cooler, although the steam still softened the air. I stared into the depths of the bath, the delicate scent filling my nose. "Come on," I whispered. "I can feel you." I stretched out my arms and watched as the little blond hairs began to rise. The buzzing started in my belly. And then the water began to ripple.

And that's when I heard it again: soft, gentle humming, a familiar melody as the water began to move more rapidly. It was the song from the dream I had weeks ago. My whole body began to tingle. My heart thumped in my chest. But there was still no image of Valerie. She stopped humming and began to sing, just a snatch of a verse. *I know where I'm going/ And I know who's going with me/ I know who I love/ And the dear knows who I'll marry.*

I listened in wonder, the words so familiar to me. The nostalgia overwhelmed me, and I felt as if I was spinning, the world around me going round and round and round.

"Mom?" I whispered. "Mother. Can you hear me?"

Suddenly, the water stilled, and a young woman appeared in profile. I held my breath. It was like watching a movie. I had a vision of Valerie as a young woman. She was wearing an oversize olive smock, her hair in a long braid that snaked down her back. She was crying, and the pain I felt was like an ache in my belly. And then the background came into view. She was outside the bakery, the Philpotts' bakery, where Gina grew up. The image was as clear as a digital photo. There was the hand-painted sign with its loaf of bread, the array of potted plants either side of the door. The window display with its usual luscious offerings of cakes, pastries, and breads was empty. The bakery must be closed. But what was Valerie doing? I leaned closer to the water.

It seemed as if she were transfixed, standing at an angle, watching the Philpotts' bakery through the window. And then I saw what she was holding. An apple box. A Somerset apple box. I clutched my chest. I knew that box. I still had it. And if my vision was true, I was tucked inside that box. I felt as though I weren't the baby in the box but the woman standing there filled with despair and loneliness.

The vision began to waver, but I realized it was my tears blurring the sight. I blinked them back.

Now the vision began to expand, growing across the surface of the water. There was Gina's dad, Gareth, arriving to open the bakery. Despite the sadness, I smiled at him. He was like a second father to me when I was a kid. And then I realized that Valerie had disappeared. I searched the scene. She was hidden behind a birch tree. I looked back to Gareth and followed his gaze. The apple box was on the step to the store. Gareth looked around, bemused. It was like I could see his brain working; *Did I make a fruit order last night?* he was thinking. And then he leant down. Gasped. Although his bent figure obscured my view, I knew he was uncovering the baby blanket, the shawl that I'd seen on the viscount's mother's portrait. He straightened, unlocked the door to the bakery, picked up the box and walked inside.

My heart was in my throat. The vision began to shimmer and fade. All the energy crashed out of my body. "How could you leave me?" I asked the water, in mourning now for that helpless baby and for the mother who I could feel was dying inside.

To my surprise, Valerie's voice answered my question.

"I tried to keep you safe. Please go. It's not safe for you here."

And the last embers of the vision disappeared.

CHAPTER 7

"*Y*our braiding is getting much neater," Ruta said.

I looked up to see my new boss looking proud. "Thanks," I said.

"Kind of surprising considering your head has been in the clouds all morning," she added, not without a shade of concern.

I'd only been working with Ruta for a week, but I'd soon realized that behind her no-nonsense approach was a kind-hearted woman. As she was ten years my senior, I got the feeling that she'd taken on a bit of a big-sister role. And there was no fooling big sis—my head *had* been in the clouds all morning. Since six a.m., in fact, when I clocked in at the inn for the breakfast prep shift. Although clouds weren't the best way to put it—more like my head had been in the water. Last night's vision hadn't left me, and I was troubled by how many unanswered questions still plagued me. My vision-mother—and was she even real, or was it really my imagination conjuring her?—had disappeared after giving yet another cryptic message.

"Why?" I'd all but shouted in the empty bathroom. "Why should I leave? Why am I in danger?"

But there was no one there. I was alone in my bathroom, and the water had gone cold. I lost my taste for a long soak and instead had a quick shower.

I thanked Ruta and turned my attention to the next batch of croissants for the inn's breakfast buffet. What Ruta didn't know was that braiding pastry was kind of a therapy for me. My fingers worked deftly and intuitively, which gave my mind freedom to roam.

Watching the moment my mother abandoned me had near broken my heart. It was some comfort to know it had also broken her heart. In the vision, I could feel every ounce of my birth mom's pain. She didn't want to leave me at the Philpotts'. The decision was tearing her apart. But she felt she had no choice. That I wasn't safe in her arms. That she couldn't protect me, not the way she wanted to, not the way mothers are supposed to protect their children.

At least she'd watched from a hiding place. She must have chosen the Philpotts. Perhaps she'd shopped at the bakery and seen the way the parents worked together with such obvious fondness. They had small children, so perhaps she believed they'd look after me or at least make certain I was cared for until the right family was found. And she'd been right. I might have been abandoned outside the bakery, but I'd never not felt loved.

Witnessing that episode of my life, which previously had only been known to me through Gareth Philpott's stories, had been difficult in a way I never could have predicted. Because instead of feeling sorry for myself, for the poor innocent baby bundled inside a blanket, I had new compassion for Valerie, for my birth mom. I'd been so caught up in trying to unravel the story behind the moment that I didn't think I'd ever stopped to consider how harrowing leaving me must have been. The specific quality of that pain felt like it had coated my bones last night; I couldn't shake myself free.

To top it all off, I still hadn't been able to get hold of Joanna. Her phone wouldn't connect, and no matter how many times I refreshed my emails, no shiny new reply from Joanna appeared...just several promotions about baking equipment and a reminder to renew my car insurance for the year. Great.

But Joanna's and Valerie's words still hung in the air. Both had warned me away from Broomewode. What did they know? Why wouldn't they share more information? Were they themselves scared? It seemed like the only logical conclusion—but why wouldn't they tell me more? I was stubborn, and until someone explained to me exactly why I was supposed to leave, I didn't feel like running away. I'd invested too much time and energy into my quest to find out where I'd come from.

I finished braiding my last all-butter croissant and moved on to almond paste for the mini Bakewell tarts Ruta wanted to serve this afternoon for her anticipated post-hunt rush. "Only the most traditional recipes today," she'd said this morning. "The hunting lot aren't after innovation. They want an authentic English countryside experience." I'd tried not to roll my eyes. Even after Benedict explained how the hunt wasn't actually going to harm any animals, the whole thing still seemed antiquated to me. I guessed I must really enjoy his company not to mind...but I wasn't going to allow my brain to start whirring over tonight's date just yet. There was too much to sort out first. For starters, whether I should actually consider leaving Broomewode Village like the women had warned.

I turned on my electric mixer and watched as the sugar and ground almonds were churned to a paste. For the first time, it struck me that maybe Joanna had been behind the warning note that was left for me at the inn all those weeks ago. But no, that didn't make sense. Joanna didn't even know who I was back then. Why would she leave a warning note? Argh. One warning I could ignore, but three? And all those near-death accidents that had befallen me since I stepped foot in the village? Without Sly, Gateau, and Joanna around, I would have been crushed as smooth as my almond paste on more than one occasion. Even Elspeth and Jonathon had told me to think twice about accepting the position at the inn. It was hard for me to articulate exactly what compelled me to stay. Despite the dangers, Broomewode called me to it, and the call was powerful. There was something here for me. The truth was here for me. I was getting closer. I just had to stay alive to discover it. Forewarned is forearmed and all that. At least, I hoped so.

With the almond paste finished, I set about rolling out the short crust pastry I'd prepared. The plan was for mini Bakewell tarts, and at Ruta's request, they had to be uniform in size. She was so excited about the hunt and the extra business it would bring to the inn. It must be a huge change of pace to be working in such a small kitchen after the rush of the capital. She was probably hungry for the pressure. I couldn't really relate.

But I worked as quickly and methodically as possible, relieved that Gerry had left me in peace for a while. He'd cornered me early this morning (so early I hadn't even managed to get started on my second cup of coffee) and demanded to know what had happened at The Hourglass café yesterday. The whole inn was talking about it, he'd said, and he had been worrying all night. "Do you know how long the night can feel when you're a ghost who no one can see?" he'd wailed. So I'd told him everything, each little detail, but then Ruta arrived, forcing me to cut my seemingly one-sided conversation short. "Later," Gerry intoned. "I'll do some snooping when the guests wake up. See if I can learn anything hovering in their rooms."

"Don't freak them out," I warned him.

"You worry too much. Everyone loves a good ghost story. I could put this place on the map."

"It's already on the map. Please," I whispered. I had enough to worry about without panicked inn guests.

"Tell you one thing," Gerry said, floating near my ear, even though no one else could hear him. "I overhead Florence last weekend on the phone. She is dead set on winning the baking competition. *Dead* set."

Normally, I'd hear a term like that and think it was pure exaggeration, but Gerry hadn't become a ghost by accident. I felt a shiver run over me. "What do you mean?" I muttered the words while looking at my recipe. Let Ruta think I was reciting the ingredients or something.

Florence and I were friends, sort of, but I never entirely trusted her. I could see her naked ambition, but so long as she won the competition fair and square, I would congratulate her with as much joy as I would feel for Hamish or Gaurav. But if she tried something underhanded, I couldn't stand by and let it happen.

Gerry jumped up on the counter and scooched so close to me, I felt a chill on my arm. "I heard her on the phone to someone. She said, 'Of course I'll win, darling,' and laughed." Here he threw back his head, tossed imaginary curls, and made a fair imitation of Florence's husky chuckle. I had to bite my lip to stop myself from laughing. He was good.

"She's building her confidence. That's all," I said, hoping it was true. Still, on top of everything else, I decided we'd better keep an eye on the beautiful Italian baker. "It wouldn't hurt to watch her carefully." I glanced over at him. "And no one does that better or more discreetly than you."

He looked so pleased that I was glad I'd asked him. At least if Gerry had a job to do, he wouldn't be quite so much in my business. At least, I hoped not.

It was warm in the kitchen, and even though I'd pinned my long, dark hair up, it felt heavy. I was thinking about seeing if Eve would make me an iced coffee when a rap at the kitchen door broke my reverie.

Ruta called out, "Hello?" and to my astonishment, Benedict walked in.

He was wearing the distinctly British hunting garb of Hunting Pink, even though it was a scarlet coat over white breeches with long leather boots. My first thought was that he must have been absolutely boiling, and then that thought was quickly replaced by the observation that he actually looked super handsome. Dashing was the word. I found myself blushing. He was destined to be the Earl of Frome one day, and I was in the kitchen, elbow-deep in flour. I definitely had a *Downton Abbey* moment where I thought that a hundred years ago, if he'd walked in, I'd have had to curtsy.

It didn't help that Gerry said, "Look who's slumming it. And Poppy, you're blushing."

And that really helped soothe my overheated features.

I didn't often think of Benedict as the future earl, but today I did. It was the confidence with which he walked, how he held himself straight-backed. He was so solid, so *present*.

"Morning," he said. "Sorry to intrude. I just came to check on you, Poppy, after yesterday. You're all right?"

Between Eve's special ointment and a good night's sleep, I felt fine, but I appreciated his concern.

"What happened yesterday?" Ruta asked, alarm filling her eyes.

I'd managed to get away without explaining yesterday's events to my boss. I didn't want her to worry or to think I wasn't up to doing my job. I frowned at Benedict.

Benedict, sensing his error, began to backtrack, but Ruta interrupted. "You weren't near that runaway tractor yesterday, were you?" She looked horrified. "Everyone was talking about it. Do you know there were two women sitting at a table right in the path of the tractor? It's a miracle they weren't killed."

Benedict nodded. "The police are investigating the crash, but it seems like the tractor was parked on the slope of a hill, which it shouldn't have been, and somehow got loose." I appreciated that by talking about the event in general, he was deflecting Ruta from asking where exactly I'd been during the incident.

"Is the farmer to blame?" I asked. "He seemed mortified, but if he parked somewhere unsafe, that's negligence, right?"

"The tractor company are also investigating the case. It's

not yet clear who is at fault. But the farmer, Riley, probably wasn't paying proper attention, embroiled as he was in an almighty row with my father yesterday."

Ah! That's who I'd seen when driving down the hill. I wasn't close enough to make out the faces, just the wild gesticulating. I should have guessed it was Robert Champney, the Earl of Frome, throwing his weight around. Sometimes it was hard to believe that Benedict shared his genes.

A delivery truck pulled up outside, and Ruta excused herself and went out.

"Do you know what the fight was about?" I asked as I began to cut my pastry into mini tartlet sizes.

Benedict casually leaned against my work surface, and Gerry mirrored his pose on the other side. I wished Gerry would go haunt someone else for five minutes.

Luckily Benedict was staring straight ahead, a slight frown crinkling his brow. "The tenant farmer, Riley, hates the hunt. Every year, it's the same struggle. He does everything in his power to keep the hunters off his farm, claiming they ruin his crops and leave gates open to let his sheep out. All of which is nonsense—no one on the hunt would disrespect the land or do anything to compromise the animals. We're all country folk. Basically, he hates my father."

"Oh dear," I murmured. It was a tale as old as time— farmer and landowner at loggerheads. "I actually drove past them arguing yesterday, though I couldn't see who it was at the time."

"Lots of wild hand gestures?" Benedict asked.

"Exactly." I laughed. "Was your father able to smooth things over?"

Benedict explained that Farmer Riley didn't have much

choice. The land belonged to his father, and he assured his tenant that the hunt wouldn't damage the farm. It was clear, though he didn't say the words, that Riley had no choice in the matter.

As he spoke, I spooned the almond paste and some cherry jam into the pastry-lined tartlet cases and began to slice fresh morello cherries. Benedict leaned over and popped one into his mouth. I swatted his hand away. "You're incorrigible." I smiled.

I asked how Benedict was going to join in on the hunt since he already knew the route.

"I won't," he said simply. "I'll just be keeping an eye on things. Make sure it runs smoothly. It's a big operation."

I nodded, trying to divide my focus between the tartlets and the sweet thing beside me. And ignore the annoying ghost who was making kissing noises. Honestly, Gerry had been immature and annoying in life, and death hadn't changed him.

"I also keep track of the schedule. I need to make sure my father gets away in time to be back at Broomewode Hall. He and Mother like to get back first to welcome their guests for the breakfast meal. Sometimes he gets carried away and forgets. Speaking of which—" Benedict looked at his watch. "I'd better get going. The hunt starts at eleven."

He lowered his voice. "You're sure you're well enough for this evening?"

Not even Gerry could spoil this moment, and he tried. I smiled at Benedict, feeling a bit shy. "I'm looking forward to it."

Relief flashed across Benedict's face. He bent down and placed a soft kiss on my left cheek. "Me, too. I'll text you later.

You should swing by the hunt if you like later. It's a wonderful sight. Very traditional, of course, though no foxes will be harmed."

I watched as Benedict disappeared through the door. I hadn't lied—I *was* looking forward to our dinner—it was just that I'd been too busy fretting over Joanna's whereabouts to give it much attention. I pulled out my phone and stared at the blank screen. Well, she knew how to return a phone call. For a couple of hours, I was determined to put Joanna out of mind and enjoy myself. Maybe I'd even crack out that red summer dress I'd bought on sale last year and never had anywhere to wear it. And Gina could do my makeup. I chuckled. I sounded like a smitten kitten.

Even Gerry floated off in disgust.

Maybe I was.

CHAPTER 8

*T*wo hours later, and the breakfast rush at the inn was the most intense I'd ever seen it. Now I knew why Ruta had been so concerned about baking so many extra croissants and she and Pavel had worked tirelessly delivering hearty meals. She'd obviously done her research and realized that as well as the landed gentry and rich socialites that would accompany the earl on the hunt, the event itself drew spectators, people who were interested in watching the dogs at work or families who liked to see the horses gallop across the trails.

In the dining room, Eve had set out extra tables and chairs to accommodate the stream of customers, which had been flowing nonstop all morning. And the demand for sugary provisions was high. I could only imagine how busy the inn would be post-hunt, full to the brim with hungry spectators desperate to satiate their appetites after a long morning following the hunt across Broomewode's hills.

I stuck my head outside the kitchen to see if Eve needed a hand. The atmosphere was electric, like nothing I'd experienced before. Despite my earlier reservations, I found myself feeling a bit interested in this age-old custom. I approached Eve, but she told me that everything was under control— she'd brought in some extra hands. Seemed like everyone but me had anticipated the popularity of the hunt.

"Why don't you check it out, luvvie," Eve suggested. "The hunt is a big part of Broomewode Village history. I'll pop up myself if I get a chance. I like to see them off."

It was a thoughtful suggestion, and I thanked Eve. "I don't suppose you've seen where Gateau's got to? She scampered off the moment I opened the car door this morning. I wish she'd at least pretend to miss me."

Eve smiled and tucked her long braid back. "Familiars have their own lives, too, you know." She was called away by a customer, so I returned to the kitchen and finished my duties. Cleaning up after myself was always such a bore.

Ruta told me to clock off before the lunch rush started. "Make the most of your break," she warned. "It's going to be chaos later; I can feel it."

I'd had enough chaos yesterday with a wayward tractor interrupting a very important coffee date. I slipped off my apron, gave my amulet a pat, and decided that I'd follow Eve's suggestion and head up to Broomewode Hall to watch the hunt gather.

Part of me was hoping that Joanna might have the same idea. Maybe she'd planned to surprise her mother yesterday and had gone to her later. Would I find her safe and well in the crowd? Clearly it was drawing all kinds of different people. Hmm, a long shot maybe, but then you never knew.

Joining the stream of customers leaving the inn, I suddenly felt self-conscious. Everyone had made a big effort for the big day out, and there were lots of bold reds and yellows to match the jackets of the riders. No one seemed to mind that it was mid-June and gloriously warm. I fell in step with a young family with what looked like boy and girl twins. The mother couldn't have been much older than me, her cheeks rosy with the effort of holding one child on her hip and the other with a spare hand. The twins were three or perhaps four years old.

The little girl caught me looking at them and smiled. She was eating a slice of watermelon, and the pink juice dribbled down her chin as she munched. Her white T-shirt was embroidered with a Dalmatian. Her brother, stuck firmly to his mom's side, was singing to himself.

I smiled back at the girl. "Are you looking forward to seeing the race?"

"The dogs go jump," the little girl said.

"Up!" agreed the boy.

The mom wiped a bead of sweat from her brow as the boy wriggled in her arms. "Personally, my favorite bit is at the end when everyone drinks sloe gin," she said with a shy smile. "But the kids love watching the hounds." She lowered her voice. "They are desperate for a p-u-p-p-y," she said, sounding out the letters.

"I like Dalmatians," the little girl said.

"Me too," I replied.

We continued up the path with the rest of the hordes, but when I turned to speak again, I realized I'd lost them along the way.

I kept walking, buoyed by the excited mood of the crowd, and soon found myself in the gorgeous grounds outside the manor house where the hunt was due to start. I had no idea what to expect. Did a horn blow? Was there a speech? What exactly were we all waiting for?

I must have looked as clueless as I felt because I heard a voice say, "I'm guessing this is your first hunt?"

I turned and saw a man in his mid-forties standing beside me wearing an outfit similar to most of the men in the crowd. He had dark hair, gray eyes, and an impressive thick mustache nestled in the middle of a doughy, friendly face. I smiled and nodded. "That obvious?"

"I'm afraid so, but fear not—I can help."

He extended a hand and introduced himself as Oliver Jones. He had a faint accent, too mild for me to place. Perhaps Scottish. "The Huntsman has emerged," he said. I followed the direction of his gaze, and there was the earl in a scarlet jacket next to a younger man who was clutching a traditional hunting horn. "That gentleman is responsible for and in charge of the hounds."

He paused and looked at me inquiringly to see if I was taking it all in.

"Got it," I replied. I guessed I'd asked to be schooled, and it was interesting.

"Good. Now see that fellow beside the Huntsman?"

I nodded.

"That's the Whipper-in. In other words, the Huntsman's right-hand man. He has an important job, too, aiding the Huntsman and helping to keep the pack of hounds together. If any stray away or get left behind, he gallops off and collects them. He also keeps the followers away from the hounds. You'd be surprised how often they forget they're just spectators."

He paused again to make sure I was paying attention.

Jeez, trust me to have found the most enthusiastic man in the audience. I made a reassuring noise.

"And the fellow beside him? That's the field master."

I smiled. He was talking about Benedict, who was wearing a similar but paler in color jacket to his father. I watched Benedict as he sat astride a chestnut-colored horse. Soon, he would be galloping across the Somerset countryside, down hills, over fences, and back up the hills again. It was strange to see him looking so formal. It reminded me of the first time I'd set eyes on him while trespassing on Broomewode Hall property. At the time, I had thought he was a ghost, destined to reenact some battle or other. Now I was going to dinner with him. That Poppy and that Benedict felt like different people. We'd come so far since then.

"Yes. He has a very important job."

I looked again at Benedict, who was now chatting away to Edward. He didn't look in the least ruffled by being surrounded by eager hunters and followers, not to mention some very excited dogs. Sorry, hounds.

"He's in charge of directing everyone else out riding," Oliver said, "and making sure they behave themselves."

"Do people misbehave at these things?" I asked. "Isn't it all gallop gallop and sniff sniff sniff with the hounds?"

The man showed me the whites in his eyes.

I swallowed. Clearly a hunt wasn't the place for humor.

"My dear, you're oversimplifying things. Lots of things can go wrong on a hunt. Some can't be helped, like an injured horse and a rider falling. But other disasters are for the field master to mitigate. It would be an unthinkable sin to damage a farmer's property or leave open a gate for his cows to wander freely."

Aha, now this I did know. It was the whole reason the earl and Farmer Riley had been arguing yesterday.

"And if that happens?"

Oliver narrowed his eyes to slits and drew a finger across his throat. "The offending rider would be sent home."

Hmm. That was not the dramatic consequence I'd imagined. It sounded more like acting up at summer camp and having your parents called to pick you up early.

"I can assure you, it's the most embarrassing thing which can happen to a rider."

Around us, the crowd was swelling. I still couldn't believe that the hunt drew such a loyal following. I was jostled as more people pushed and elbowed their way to the front.

"Stand firm," Oliver instructed. "You don't want to lose this spot. We've got a prime position."

He pointed now to the growing number of horses arriving on the scene. It looked to be at least thirty riders. I had to admit it was an impressive sight: all the men and some women, too, in their traditional regalia, the fine horses groomed and shining. I could see why this was the preferred sport of the wealthy. Getting all the kit together must have cost the riders a fortune. The jackets and shirts and the incredibly fancy-looking boots. Not to mention the expense of the horse's upkeep—the vet's bills alone would be burning a hole in my baker's apron.

"What are their funny hats called?" I asked.

"Pateys," he said with a blustery chuckle. "Don't let a rider hear you say that. They're *very* vain about the uniform."

I turned to see Oliver Jones looking at me and realized he wanted to know what I thought.

"It's all very impressive," I said. "But how do you know so much about the hunt?"

He drew himself up to his full height and lightly ran his thumb over his mustache. "I specialize in selling horses especially for hunting. Family business, has been for years. We source the best specimens from Scotland. The hunters there are famous. No other breeder can match their strength, stamina, and jumping ability. We sell them worldwide. All across Europe and America."

"Wow," I said. "How lucky to have found someone on the inside to explain this all to me."

The man beamed. I'd finally said the right thing.

"It's a tough business but an exhilarating one. The hunt has changed a lot, of course, since my grandpapa began trading. There's too much emphasis on how the horses look nowadays and not enough on how they ride." He shook his head. "But the scene is growing in popularity. Newcomers love the etiquette and the camaraderie."

"And the sloe gin," I added.

The man smiled. "Now you're catching on. I can't pretend the party atmosphere isn't important, too. It's a fun community. And wait until you see the horses fly across the fields and start jumping hedges. Nothing like it."

I noticed a Land Rover full of men slowly making its way along a nearby lane. "Aha, I see you've spied the Fencemenders. They're on call, as such, to mend any fences ruined by the jumps."

"They really think of everything," I murmured.

The crowd had quietened, and I could see the earl was preparing to make a speech. He looked completely in his element. Now I saw that the countess had joined him on a pure white horse. Her snowy hair was pulled into a chignon, and she was wearing a red riding suit with shining black boots. I noticed a lack of helmet and figured she'd put it on later once everyone had seen her fancy up-do. Although I hadn't endured many encounters with the countess, she certainly hadn't endeared herself to me. Dismissive and terribly full of herself, that was the impression I'd always come away with. Even now her head was held impossibly high.

The earl thanked everyone for attending and began acknowledging those involved in the hunt, a list so long and so full of jargon I tuned out. To my amusement, I wasn't the only one not paying attention. Edward and Benedict appeared to be sharing a whispered joke. I grinned. I still couldn't believe that we were going to be eating dinner together this evening. Alone. In a restaurant. On a date.

Finally, the earl seemed like he was wrapping things up. "And as Otto von Bismarck so brilliantly put it—men never lie so much as after a hunt, during a war, or before an election."

While the crowd tittered at the quote, I felt a jab in my ribs turn my attention away. It was Trim, the reporter from the local paper, and he leaned in and whispered, "He quotes Bismarck every year and always gets it wrong."

I had to laugh. Unlike the majority of the men in the crowd, Trim was wearing a white shirt with the sleeves rolled halfway up his arms and a pair of tan slacks as usual. He was sweating profusely and wiped a handkerchief across his temples. An enormous Canon digital camera hung around his neck. I'd had my eye on that exact model but balked at the price. "You covering the hunt?"

"Oh yes, it's big Broomewode news." He lowered his voice again. "I usually follow along in the car for some good action shots. I've just been taking photos of the earl. Now there's a man who's fussy about lighting. He knows his angles, if you know what I mean."

I giggled again. Trim was certainly providing the comic relief to my schooling from Oliver. I introduced the two men, and they shook hands solemnly. I explained that Oliver was a breeder, and Trim asked if he could take his photo—an offer to which Oliver glowed and said he was happy to oblige. As the two men negotiated the light, I watched as the hunt's strange ceremony continued. Wine and fruitcake were being passed out among the riders on horseback by the Champneys' butler and a footman.

Photo shoot over, Oliver declared he had to "talk business" with a few of the men who'd come up from London before the hunt began. I thanked him for sharing his knowledge and watched as he disappeared into the crowd.

"I heard you were at Larkville yesterday, when the tractor crashed into the café," Trim said.

My heart sank. Of course, the local reporter would discover I'd been at the scene of a local disaster. "I was," I agreed. Not wishing to be interviewed about my experience, I decided to ask a question instead. "Do you know anything about what happened?"

He shook his head. "Police are still investigating." He looked annoyed. "Working for a local paper, I barely get a phone call returned. I can tell you one thing, though. The farmer is trying to blame the earl." He kept his voice low, as well he might, since we were in front of Broomewode Hall and the earl was happily chatting away to the fellow hunters.

I also kept my voice low. "How is a runaway tractor the earl's fault?"

He shook his head. "No idea. He's claiming Robert Champney is trying to get rid of him and caused the accident to make him look bad. Of course, they hate each other, those two. It's colorful, but I won't even print that kind of accusation. I don't need a libel suit."

"Can't the earl just refuse to renew his lease if he's a tenant farmer?" I was pretty fuzzy on British law, and Trim shook his head again.

"Nathaniel Riley's family have farmed that land for generations. It would be extremely difficult to get rid of him." He looked at the earl, his eyes narrowed. "Though if it turns out Riley's blamed for that accident..." He seemed to mull the possibilities. "No. It's ridiculous." Then his attention was caught by the hunt preparing to depart. "Look at those horses," he breathed. "Aren't they fantastic? I have to admit, I do find the whole thing really exciting. Shame it's such an expensive sport, else I might get more involved myself. There's a local hunt club, mostly made up of followers who'll watch the hunt by car or foot. They often organize fundraising events to support the hunt. And I know the main Master of the Hunt, Charles Radlier, quite well. Interviewed him several times."

"The Master? Not the Field Master?" I repeated, feeling quite lost again in all the jargon.

"The Master's in charge of the finances raised by the hunt club. A very important role since this"—he paused and grandly swung an arm around—"is not cheap."

"I can imagine," I said, utterly bemused.

Edward had spied me in the crowd and, now dismounted from his horse, was waving and making his way over.

"Poppy, so glad to see you up and about. How you feeling after yesterday's near miss?"

"I'm fine," I said quietly. I'd deflected Trim's attention, and now it was back.

"Look, I can't stop now, but I'm doing a follow-up story on the accident. I'd love to speak with you. Catch you after the hunt."

Before I could decline to be interviewed, Trim excused himself to get his ride with the top "car followers" for the hunt, and Edward said he had to get back to the hounds.

The excitement outside the manor house was mounting, the crowd jostling and the horses restive. As I was wondering when the darned thing would actually start, I saw Katie Donegal at the edge of the earl's group. She was clutching a piece of paper and frowning.

I pushed my way through the crowd, intent on asking her if she'd told anyone that I was heading to the coffee shop yesterday after she'd seen me at Susan's.

I called her name, and Katie looked up. She was still frowning, and I saw now that her usually neat bun was losing its pins, stray gray tendrils escaping down her neck. The paper she clutched in both hands was a schedule, and Katie was red in the face and clearly overwhelmed.

I said hello and asked how she was doing, but Katie only replied with a shake of the head, as if to say, *Goodness me, girlie, can't you see I'm stressed?* She ran a finger over the schedule.

"I can see you're busy, but I was just wondering if you mentioned to anyone I'd be at The Hourglass yesterday?"

Katie's frown deepened. She looked at me as if I was speaking another language. "Sorry, dearie, I can't stay and chitchat." She brandished the mucky piece of paper in front of me. "I've a strict schedule to keep, and I'm barely keeping my head on straight!"

I looked at the schedule and could see why. Katie's looping handwriting sprawled across the whole page like the pen in her hand had gone dancing. The entire day was timed to the minute. A few things jumped out at me. Seven a.m., brew the coffee. (The word coffee always drew my eye.) Twelve, sausages and bacon. One forty-five, fetch champagne from cellar for earl's return.

I raised an eyebrow. "Who needs their champagne at exactly one forty-five p.m.?"

"The earl, dearie. He's very precise. He runs his hunt like a military campaign, and I must work to schedule."

Before I could reply, the almighty cry of a Klaxon ripped through the air. Hounds began to bark. Horses were on the move. The hunt had begun. I turned to comment on the sight, but Katie was already walking back up to the manor house, the rest of her bun unraveling in the breeze.

CHAPTER 9

I couldn't help but wonder at Katie's strange behavior. She hadn't been herself lately: skittish, evasive, withdrawn. Was it simply that she was overworked? That looking after Mitty and keeping Broomewode Hall's kitchen in order was becoming too much? Although usually full of energy, Katie was surely close to retirement age. But something was niggling at me, an unpleasant, tricksy thought. She could have overheard me talking to Susan about my coffee date. And I couldn't overlook how difficult she'd made talking to Mitty. It was as if she was protecting him from *me* somehow. But what possible threat could I present?

Break over, I headed back to the inn. As I walked down the path, I caught sight of the competition tent, with the techs busily at work getting ready to shoot the semifinal episode of *The Great British Baking Contest.* For a quiet village, there was a lot going on in Broomewode.

I got back to find Ruta busily preparing for the late lunch crowd. I told her and Pavel about the scene I'd witnessed while I carried on with my afternoon cakes.

I had a lot on my mind and jumped when Ruta called, "Hey, dreamy." I looked down to see I'd spread too much chocolate ganache on the sponge cake.

"I told you these hunting folk had appetites. I was thinking, we did so well on picnic boxes for those who want to eat outside that we might start offering them every weekend. What do you think? You'd need to make cookies or small cakes that could be packed in a picnic lunch."

"Wow." I was impressed by Ruta's savvy. She'd spotted a new market for us. It wasn't something the inn had done before, but it made so much sense. As I scraped off some of the chocolate ganache, I told her I'd be happy to work on picnic-friendly goodies. For now, I had to get my head in gear and make sure we had enough baked goods to go round this afternoon after the hunt finished. Katie Donegal wasn't the only one with a lot of cooking to do today.

I kept my head down, and before long I'd baked my little heart out and we had enough cakes for what was sure to be a manic late lunch rush.

Ruta thanked me for working so hard. I told her it was my pleasure. We were a great team. She handed me a cold roast chicken sandwich with crisp iceberg lettuce and homemade mayo. "Now go sit down and eat something," Ruta commanded. "I'll join you in a bit."

I gratefully took my sandwich and headed to the bar, where I was hoping to catch Eve and ask if she'd noticed anything strange about Katie Donegal lately. But of course, Gerry decided this was his moment to crash into me as he somersaulted through the kitchen doors.

"The contestants have arrived!" he trilled. "So early. It's semifinal showdown weekend."

I was as excited as Gerry, who sounded as excited as if he'd made it to the final himself. The contestants usually arrived Friday night but they must have decided to come early enough for lunch.

Gerry kept up his chatter as we entered the pub. His bets were on Florence "for being so gorgeous and winning the hearts of the nation as well as their stomachs." Then he said in a lower voice, "Besides being willing to stop at nothing to win."

I wasn't so sure myself. Each contestant had different attributes that made their baking special. I didn't believe a winner could be crowned on their looks or personality alone. It had to be about their talent as a baker. Although I had to keep these thoughts to myself. The pub was busy. Clearly not everyone in Broomewode followed the hunt. And I couldn't be seen talking to myself.

I scanned the pub until I spotted the bakers sitting around a circular table by the window.

"Hey!" I called out, thrilled to see them.

Gaurav, Florence, and Hamish looked up and waved me over. They were smiling, but their eyes told a different story. They were three bundles of nerves. I recognized the tense shoulders and stiffness of a body that had spent hours bent over a hot stove stirring up some innovative creations—with mixed success. Getting ready for the weekend was more work, well, than work itself.

"They look more like ghosts than I do!" Gerry exclaimed.

I tried not to smile. Gerry had hit the nail on the head. They were paler than I'd ever seen.

I pulled up a chair, happy to see my friends even if I didn't know how to soothe their tension. I put on a bright smile and asked everyone the dreaded question: "How are you?"

The response was mixed. Florence flicked back her extra-bouncy curls and flashed her white teeth. "Happy to see you," she said, leaning over to kiss both my cheeks. "It's been quite the week of nerves." I squeezed her hand and told her she'd be fine. She was wearing a strappy maxi dress with tiny strawberries dotted across the white cotton.

"But obviously this being chocolate week is a relief for me. I simply adore all chocolate, and Italian chocolate is quite superior."

Hamish caught my eye and shot me a cheeky look. He was wearing a navy T-shirt and a smart pair of indigo jeans. "We Scots have some fine chocolate too. It's not all deep-fried Mars bars."

Gaurav smiled too, but I could see it was an effort. "I've been practicing all week, but chocolate is really not my thing. I don't like eating it myself unless it has a very high cacao content, like ninety percent. The more bitter, the better. It's difficult to know what's good for other people. Milk chocolate, white chocolate. I don't understand it at all." He rubbed his temple nervously and then rolled up his shirtsleeves like he was about to start baking again.

Gerry turned somersaults in the air and then floated over to Florence, leaning over her shoulder to pretend to drink her coffee.

I assured Gaurav that it was understanding the science of how flavor worked rather than enjoying the product that made a good baker.

Hamish agreed. "You can't like everything."

I bit into my sandwich and listened as they discussed

their signature chocolate bakes. Each of them had created a recipe that represented their personality. Florence's was rich and complicated, Hamish more adventurous with the use of coffee and spices, and Gaurav was sticking to a pretty traditional recipe. I guessed he was afraid of messing things up if he experimented too much.

Although I could feel how much the competition meant to each of them, Hamish was stoic in his approach. "At the end of the day, I've tried my best, and no one can do more than that. I'm happy to have made it this far. Me mam certainly thinks I'm a winner already. She's dead proud."

I took the last bite of my sandwich and then told Hamish his attitude was the best antidote to stress. "All of you have come so far," I said. "You're winners in my eyes. But one thing I do know is that you have to relax before the show tomorrow. You can't stay a bundle of nerves. It's bad for your health!"

I paused. What could I do to take the bakers' minds off the competition?

"Tell you what," I said. "I have the perfect distraction from this weekend." I explained about the hunt, how it was a traditional part of Broomewode Village life and not cruel at all—more like a day out for families and horse lovers. I checked my watch. It was 1:20 p.m. "It should be coming to a close very soon," I said, recalling Katie's schedule and the champagne being fetched from the cellar at 1:45 p.m. The earl would show up soon and then the rest of the hunt shortly after. The whole thing was so well-choreographed, presumably so he could serve the perfect, unspoiled breakfast right on schedule. Oh, the lives of the rich and titled.

"If we walk up now, we'll catch them coming," I suggested. "The start was more exciting than I'd thought it'd be. You'll enjoy seeing the horses and the riders dressed in hunt gear. And the hounds are lovely."

"Great," Gerry drawled sarcastically. "It took you all of five minutes to devoid me of company." He clapped his hands together without making a sound.

"Why, I'd clean forgotten the hunt was today!" Hamish said. "I would love to go and watch."

Although Florence looked less than impressed. "I'm surprised I wasn't invited to take part," she said, and I could see she pictured herself in full riding gear on horseback, the center of attention, rather than slogging across the fields on foot with the rest of us. However, since we were all going, she decided to come along.

Eve waved as we left—I'd have to wait until later to talk to her about Katie Donegal. Right now, my friends needed me.

After the rush this morning, it was eerily quiet. The hunting crowds were out on horseback, walking the fields or following in cars, and now the sound of chirping birds broke through the sky. I squinted past the glare of the sun and looked into the blue for signs of the hawk. Nothing. I took it as a good sign. No stray tractors about to crash into me...or whatever else the universe felt like chucking my way.

Somewhere in the distance, a dog barked, but I wasn't sure if it was a hunting hound or a local dog.

As we walked the path back toward the manor house, I put a ban on any talk of the competition, but before I even finished the sentence, Hamish began to wax lyrical about trail hunting. It hadn't even occurred to me that he saw a lot of hunts where he lived in the Highlands, but of course it made perfect sense. He was a nature man as well as a policeman.

Gaurav looked bemused as Hamish tried to explain the different cries used by the Huntsman. "Obviously it's different for different hunts," Hamish said, "but traditionally you might hear "hark," "forrard," or "Tally-ho!"

Florence looked at me and giggled. "You're joking, right?" she asked Hamish, looking as incredulous as she would if someone questioned the quality of her pasta-making skills.

"Nope, deadly serious," Hamish replied. "The huntsmen used to use those sounds to get the foxes moving. Obviously nowadays that's moot—there's no fox—but part of the showmanship still exists, and the hounds respond to the commands. Once the hounds are on a scent and away out of the covert, the Huntsman signals to the Master, using the horn, and the field gallops on after."

"It's so complicated," I mused. "I'll never keep up with all the names and jargon. I don't know how you remember it all."

"How does this all work if it's raining?" Gaurav asked.

I smiled. Ever the technical brain.

"Good question," Hamish noted. "Hunting can happen in all weathers unless it's so bad the horses might get injured, say if the ground is frozen over or it's way too wet."

"And if it gets dark?" Gaurav asked.

"The hunt will pack up if it begins to get too dark out. Some hardy huntsmen, especially in Scotland, will carry on hunting on foot in snow, and it is fairly common for a determined hunt to just decide to keep going."

"Yeesh," I said. "Not for the fainthearted."

We turned the corner and saw that the crowds had begun to flow back to Broomewode Hall. As we joined them, Florence looked disappointed. "It looks like a lot of hanging around," she said, shrugging. "And where are the handsome men?"

I assured her they were on their way back.

I spotted my friend Oliver from earlier in the hunt and waved him over. After introducing him to the group, I asked him what had happened while I'd been back at the inn.

"You mean, since eleven a.m.?" Oliver laughed. "*Everything* has happened, Poppy, everything. It's been a thrilling hunt. So after the meet, the bit you saw, the hunt moved off to the first *covert* to be *drawn*." He emphasized the words using air quotes. "Which was across the fields." He pointed in the direction of the next village.

I shot Hamish a look that said *Help me—translate!*

"It just means they rode off across those fields," Hamish said. "A covert is a bit of scrub or trees where the fox hides."

"That's right. The Huntsman and hounds led the trail, and they were followed by the Master and the field. The hounds were encouraged by the Huntsman, who used his voice and his horn to encourage them to explore and sniff out the fox scent on the trail. And then from there it was all go go go."

Hamish asked a bunch of technical questions that made as much sense to me as listening to Greek. Gaurav lost interest, too, and whipped out his phone.

Just as I could tell Florence was going to suggest heading off for a glass of wine or a spot of shopping, something in the crowd shifted.

"What's going on?" I asked Oliver. "Why is everyone moving backwards?"

Before he could answer, a terrible scream rent the air. One long ripping breath. A collective gasp. The sound of hooves.

And then there was the countess on her white horse, her white hair escaping its chignon, her face frantic.

"Help us, help us!" she screamed.

"What's happened?" Hamish called back.

"It's the earl! He fell and hit his head. Please help. I don't know what to do!"

Hamish and I, both so intimately attuned to disaster, automatically began running behind the countess's horse.

The hounds were baying, and in the distance, we saw the huntsmen's horses on a path away from us. But there was one horse who had strayed from the pack. It stood on its hind legs, whinnying and rising up into the air. The sound was terrible. Pure distress.

"He's there!" the countess screeched. "Oh, my poor husband. My darling."

"Have you called an ambulance?" Hamish asked, ever practical. But the countess was babbling, clearly in shock. Gaurav, his phone already in hand, made the call.

Hamish and I slowed our pace and saw a body bent at an unnatural angle over a rock. I gasped, suddenly rooted to the spot, afraid of what I might see if I went closer. The body wasn't moving, eerily still. Hamish put his hand on my shoulder. "I'll check his pulse," he said quietly.

The earl's horse stopped whinnying and came to where the earl lay.

The countess dismounted from her horse. She turned her eyes away from the sight of her husband's body and up to the sky as if searching for another scenario in the skies. Her breath came in jagged bursts, and I could feel my heart beating faster, faster, hoping beyond hope that the earl was merely unconscious. That the angle of his body looked worse than it actually was.

The countess crumpled, her knees giving way until she sank to the grass. She wailed, and the sound pierced my heart. She had covered her face with her hands, her body folded into the shape of a clam.

I sat beside her on the grass, hoping it would help her feel less alone. How to comfort a woman whose husband had just suffered a terrible fall? She was a stranger to me, yet we were bound in some way through our shared history at Broomewode Hall. I placed a hand on her back so she'd know I was there but immediately recoiled. My hand had turned cold, like I'd suddenly plunged it into ice water. Was this me feeling her pain? The cold cruelness of whatever tragedy had just occurred? It sent shudders down my spine.

"I can't bear it," she said, suddenly jumping to her feet. "Robert. Robert! I can't bear it!" She rushed back to her horse and swung her lithe body over the saddle.

"Wait," I called out in vain. I watched in horror as she galloped away, back toward the manor house.

I turned and saw Hamish bending over the earl's body. I watched, silent with dread, as he gently placed two fingers on the side of the earl's neck.

A beat of silence, and then another, and another.

Hamish raised his head, a deep sadness etched onto his face. "There's no pulse. He's gone."

CHAPTER 10

*H*amish slowly walked over to me, his head hung low. I nodded grimly. While we'd been here, I'd been aware of activity back at the Hall. It sounded like the hunt was back. But without its master.

Then there was the distinct sound of a lone horse galloping toward us, coming from the opposite direction to the Hall. I stood and turned, holding my hand to my eye to shield the sun. It was Benedict, astride his chestnut horse, kicking her flanks to go faster.

He was with us in seconds, and I realized that in a moment I'd have to tell him something terrible. A shiver went through me. How would I find the words?

Benedict pulled at the reins and jumped down from the horse the moment she slowed.

"I thought I heard my mother scream." He was looking around, no doubt thinking it was the countess who'd had an accident.

"It's your father," I said quietly.

His eyes followed mine as I turned toward where his father lay dead.

Benedict stood completely still for a moment. All color drained from his face.

"I'm so sorry," I said. "I'm—"

But Benedict didn't wait for me to finish. He walked over to the earl's body. "He's fallen from his horse. Has an ambulance been called?" He sounded curt and in control, but I imagined the truth was sinking in. The earl was too still.

Hamish said, "I'm afraid he's dead."

"I can't believe it," Benedict said. He sat beside his father's body on the rock and smoothed the hair from his face.

As much as I had disliked the earl, compassion flooded through me as I watched Benedict tenderly touch his father's brow. I turned away from such an intensely private moment.

Hamish came to my side, and Gaurav checked his phone and said the police shouldn't be long.

Benedict joined us. "I don't understand," he said. "What could have happened? He was nearly back at the Hall. He was a masterful rider." He looked at the horse, but it stood near the earl, giving no clue as to what had happened.

"The ambulance is on its way," Hamish said. It didn't answer Benedict's question, but what answer was there?

Benedict continued, "He took pride in his control over the horses." He was so pale, worryingly so, and he appeared to be years older. He looked around for his mother and asked where she was. I had to explain that after leading us to the earl, she had been too upset to watch as Hamish checked for a pulse. "I think she rode back to the Hall," I said quietly. "I don't think she could cope."

I couldn't blame the countess for not being able to stay

with her dead husband. It had obviously been a terrible shock. Perhaps she'd even witnessed the fall. How awful.

Benedict just blinked at me. The shock was setting in. "Has someone called..." he started but then trailed off.

"Police are on their way," Hamish replied.

"Police?" Benedict looked confused. "But he had an accident. Fell off his horse."

"Nevertheless, sir, in a sudden death, the police are always called as well as the ambulance."

I wondered if Hamish had even noticed he'd addressed Benedict as sir. He'd naturally fallen into the role of cop.

"I'm so sorry," Gaurav said to Benedict.

Benedict lowered his head and thanked him. "The more I think about it, the more it just doesn't make sense," he said. "My father was an excellent rider. His horse, Fallion, experienced. He's been trained on these grounds and gone on dozens of hunts. Perhaps Father was tired and not paying attention."

The earl hadn't been an old man, but he hadn't been young, either. Late fifties or so, I'd guess. I wondered if he'd had a stroke or heart attack. Maybe poor Fallion hadn't had anything to do with his death.

Hamish walked back to the area where the earl had fallen, looking for something that might have tripped the horse.

I joined him, hoping to find a clue. I agreed with Benedict that the facts didn't add up. Something here was amiss.

Hamish stared at the earl. "Was he missing a button?" he asked Benedict.

I looked at the earl's coat and saw that despite its otherwise pristine appearance, the second button was missing from the chest. A loose black thread dangled in the breeze.

"No," Benedict said. "I don't think so. My father was very fussy about his clothing. It must have come off when he fell."

"It could be an important clue," I said. "Can anyone see a black wool button on the ground?"

The group scattered and began to search the area.

With my head down, scanning the sun-bleached grass, I could begin to process what had just happened. What a horrible two days. I felt wretched. My heart ached for Benedict and his loss. But my miserable thoughts were broken as I heard Gaurav cry out.

"Got it!" Gaurav was standing about ten feet away toward the Hall, off the path, below a tree.

Hamish told him not to touch it. "We don't want to contaminate any evidence with your fingerprints."

I felt Benedict by my side. "What does he mean, evidence?"

I rested my hand on his arm. "Hamish is a police officer. He's trying to work out what happened."

Benedict nodded solemnly and was about to speak when we heard the sounds of another horse galloping toward us.

As the horse came closer, the man's features sharpened. It was Charles Radlier, the man who Oliver had pointed out to me as the Master of the hunt. I conveyed this to the group as he pulled his horse to a stop.

Charles Radlier had a sharp nose, close-set blue eyes, and a high forehead. He looked to be in his late forties and was clearly besieged by stress. "What's happened here?" he asked, staring down at us from astride his splendid horse.

Hamish stepped forward and explained that the earl had

tumbled from his horse and hit his head on a rock. "It was a fatal accident, I'm afraid. The police are on their way."

Charles's eyes widened with horror. "The earl? Fallen? Surely not. Why, I've been riding alongside him for most of the hunt. He was absolutely fine. No troubles whatsoever. Sturdy as old boots."

He was clearly upset, in shock most likely, like poor Benedict. Yet it was true. One moment the earl was safely riding, the next dashed to the ground.

Charles shook his head and gave Benedict a solemn look. "What shall I tell the hunters?" He paused, the full weight of what was happening now dawning on him. "And...your mother?"

Benedict drew himself to his full height and took a deep breath. "I must go. I want to be the one to tell Mother. Go on ahead and tell them I'm on my way. Don't say anything else."

Charles nodded.

Benedict said, "I need a minute to get my head straight. Will you lead Thunder back to the stables?" He gestured at his chestnut horse, which was happily chomping the long grass. "I'll walk back."

"Anything. Whatever you need."

"Will you walk with me, Poppy?" Benedict asked.

"Of course. I'm so sorry," I said softly, taking Benedict's hand in mine.

Benedict looked down at where our fingers curled around each other and squeezed softly. "I don't know how I'm going to tell Mother. They were such a team, you see. He never made a decision without discussing it with her, and she was the same. She'll be devastated."

I understood. Benedict had suddenly found himself man

of the house, and he had to act in his mom's best interests. My heart ached for Benedict and even for the countess.

He took the first step toward the Hall, and I fell into step beside him. His hand gripped mine, and the way our fingers slotted together felt like they'd been made to fit that way. It was only a five-minute walk, but Benedict seemed to need to talk, to process what had happened.

"My father and I didn't always see eye to eye. We're different men. Our relationship was complicated at times."

Benedict looked straight ahead as he talked, his profile sharp with grief. Broomewode Hall came into view, our path heading back to that long-standing building with all its history and legacy passed down through the generations.

"It's never straightforward with family. There's always something." *Like twenty-five years of mystery, an energy vortex, and a coven of witches to discover.*

Benedict nodded. "I wonder if he was ill. This morning he was so agitated and snapped my head off. Something had obviously bothered him, but I didn't even ask. I imagined something about the hunt had displeased him. He was fixated on precision. Liked to keep to a schedule, and with the hunt, that's easily thrown. But what if it was something else? What if he wasn't feeling well and should never have ridden? I should have asked him. Perhaps he had a stroke or a heart attack and if I'd convinced him to lie down he'd still be here."

I'd had the same thought about a sudden illness, but I also knew it was useless for Benedict to beat himself up.

I stopped walking, forcing Benedict to do the same. We were almost at the manor house, and no way was I going to let him go on thinking any of this was his fault. I told him exactly that. "We never really know what's going on beneath the surface," I said. "Even if you had asked your father, you've no way of knowing if he even would have told you the truth. If the hunt was so important to him, he'd have convinced both of you he was feeling fine even if he wasn't. You can't blame yourself."

"I know you're right, Poppy, but the very least I could have done was try to get him to talk about whatever was bothering him. Maybe I could have eased his troubles."

I wished I could ease Benedict's troubles. And save him from what he now had to do.

Tell the countess that her beloved husband was dead.

CHAPTER 11

*A*t the Hall, the atmosphere had changed. Only this morning, the air had been electric with the anticipation of the hunt. All excitement and thrill for the day. Now all was subdued, people unsettled and a feeling of tension and nervousness in the air. The hunters were milling around, pacing and asking questions, baffled by the wait. The earl should have returned, the hunt concluded, and breakfast announced. But instead here was the countess, emerging from the servants' entrance, hanging on to Katie Donegal. Her hair had tumbled entirely from her bun, and she was weeping.

"She knows already," Benedict said, letting his hand fall from mine. "She can feel it, I'm sure."

My hand, warm from where our skin had pressed together, now felt cool.

The countess rushed over to where we were standing. It was difficult to tell when she had spotted us. Had she seen us holding hands? Perhaps she was too caught up in grief to notice.

"Is he...?" the countess asked, her eyes searching her son's eyes wildly. "Is he badly hurt? I was a few minutes behind him, and when I came around the corner, he was on the ground. I ran for help. I—I—tell me he's all right."

He brought his mother closer and quietly told her that the earl was dead.

She stared at him as though he might be lying, then threw herself on Benedict's chest, weeping wildly.

It was so quiet, and every eye was on the new widow. "Oh, no, my poor, poor Robert," she cried.

Then the countess drew back from Benedict, reached out her arms, and cradled his face in her palms. "And you're the earl now, my son. You're Lord Frome."

Benedict shivered beneath his mother's touch and stood back. "It's too soon for all that." He looked horrified.

The countess raised her face, tears running in rivulets down her cheeks and dropping from her jawline. Despite the sadness embedded in her features, the sagging of the mouth, the drooping of her shoulders, there was something firm and set in her eyes. "He died in the saddle; it's how dear Robert would have wanted to go. And so, the title passes. It's as it should be, my love. The king is dead. Long live the king."

She stepped away and then gave him a little push. "Go and speak to your people."

I inhaled sharply. The countess was talking as if this was the Middle Ages or something and Benedict was heir to the royal kingdom. As if nothing had changed since the reign of Henry the Eighth. It sounded like madness to me. I mean, these were not "his people." They were just other posh people who were hungry and wondering about the holdup for breakfast.

I could sense that Benedict was deeply uncomfortable. He was still in shock, too, still processing. But still, he obeyed his mother's wishes, hugging her one last time and then walking toward the group of hunters and followers hanging around, not knowing what to do with themselves.

He said in a clear voice, loud enough to carry, "I'm sorry to have to tell you that the earl has suffered a fatal accident. My father is dead."

Murmurs went up from the group, and I could hear several questions being asked at once but not the distinct words. Benedict took a deep breath—I could see his chest rise, then fall dramatically.

Katie Donegal was still standing by the servants' entrance. She looked distraught. Her hands were still clutching the schedule, and she raised it to her face, whether to hide her tears or find some solace in the earl's last instructions, I wasn't sure.

People were milling around, paying their respects. Benedict looked around and seemed to come to a decision. "Breakfast has been prepared, and you are very welcome to stay and eat." He paused. "I know it's what my father would have wanted."

People dithered, unsure about the invitation. Eating a lavish breakfast at the home of someone who had literally just died seemed a tone-deaf response to tragedy, yet I believed Benedict when he said that it was what his father would have wanted. The day had been so intricately planned, every detail thought of and executed with precision.

Now it was my turn to be unsure of what to do. I didn't want to leave Benedict alone, but I was also increasingly aware that this wasn't my family, this wasn't my world. Benedict wasn't even a guy who'd one day be an earl. As his mother had reminded all of us, he now was the earl.

I looked back to Katie, but she was all but smothered by the countess, who was clinging to her apron, her face buried against the cook's shoulder. Benedict approached me. He was remarkably composed, but I could tell how much he was suffering on the inside.

"Poppy, Katie is comforting my mother. I wonder, if it's not too much trouble, if you could help me with the breakfast? That is, unless you have to get back to the inn?"

"Of course," I said quickly. My shift was all but finished. I'd text Ruta, who I was certain would understand. "I want to help any way I can."

He nodded and thanked me. Then strode off to the next task. I didn't know how he managed to hold it together, but he was taking charge of a truly terrible situation.

Katie was still holding her precious schedule, but it was pretty clear that her priority was the countess, who still sobbed against her shoulder. Poor Katie looked sad and exhausted. I whispered that I was going to help, and with her free hand, she passed me her schedule. She looked to be in shock like the rest of the family. She said, over the countess's shoulder, "I didn't have time to get all of the champagne out of the cellar. There are still six bottles to be collected from the vault."

I told her not to worry. I doubted there'd be a lot of champagne needed today.

"Is Belinda working?" I asked, hoping that she'd be there to show me the ropes. I could really do with some help from someone who knew the kitchen.

Katie nodded. "Yes, dearie, you just ask her for anything you need. I must look after my lady."

I nodded, and as she led the countess toward the main part of the house, I made my way through the servants' entrance, apprehensive about whether I was really up to the task of getting a hunting breakfast for the masses out of the kitchen and into the dining room. But knowing Belinda was there to help soothed my worry. Belinda was a fellow witch, a few years older than me, who worked in the Broomewode kitchen. She had shiny black hair, dark, lively eyes, and a broad smile.

I walked through the hallway and came out into the great kitchen. Unlike the last time I'd been here, the kitchen was bustling, and the sound of metal spoons clanging against pots and pans and the clunk of heavy knives on wooden chopping boards filled the air. The kitchen was uncomfortably warm, the air thick with steam and fragrant with sizzling sausages and buttery eggs. There were eight members of staff in the kitchen, each busy with their duties. No wonder Katie kept such a tight hold on her schedule. I had no idea how she managed to lead a team this large. I could barely lead Gateau to a bowl of roast chicken. I gulped. The whole thing was an enterprise, and now here I was in place of Katie, its mastermind.

I spotted Belinda immediately, her shiny hair catching the light, but maybe there was a spark of electricity in the air, too, drawing me to her. She was rushing around, running from one pan and pot on the industrial stove to another, stirring and tasting. Beside her, a woman was frantically slicing sourdough bread, ready for the industrial line of toasters. I called Belinda's name, and she turned to face me, relief on her face.

"Oh, it's you, Poppy!"

And then her face fell. "Have you heard?"

I nodded grimly and then explained that Benedict had asked me to lend a hand so Katie could comfort the countess.

"Right you are," she said, wiping her brow with a tea towel. "Glad to have you. Could you help Beatrice there slicing the bread? And then we're going to have to start plating up. The more hands, the better." She gestured at the great oak table laden with silver serving platters.

I swallowed hard as the sounds of sirens filled the air. But cutting bread? That I could do. At least I didn't have to bake it.

I introduced myself to Beatrice, an older woman with lovely ginger curls, and she handed me a bread knife. "You wouldn't believe how much toast these people eat after a hunt," she muttered. "And we have to cut them in triangles. Triangles!"

Beatrice hadn't seen me on a lazy Sunday morning, happily buttering my sixth slice of toast, but hey. I was happy to help.

I got slicing and, when that was done, checked Katie's list. It looked like everyone was on schedule. And then I remembered she'd told me that she hadn't gotten all the champagne from the cellar. Argh. Would it have enough time to chill before the corks were popped? Would they even need it?

But Katie had been so concerned about the last bottles of champagne, I thought I'd better fetch them. If they weren't needed, they could go back, but at least I'd have followed her schedule.

I asked Belinda for cellar directions, and she told me to

follow the corridor toward the old pantry and I'd see a set of stairs on the left.

The pantry gave me major envy. It was a perfect square, with a flagstone floor and brick walls that kept all the produce the Champneys liked to keep stocked up on nice and cool. I'd been surprised how plentiful everything was—no doubt the wine cellar would be as lavish. The earl had liked to entertain and impress.

I passed the pantry and then took the stone stairs down to the cellar. I was kind of creeped out—a darkened cellar was so not the ideal place to visit after today's terrible accident— but I owed it to Katie. And Benedict.

But the moment I set foot in the cellar, an automatic light sensor flicked on. "Fancy," I said, taking in the sight before me. It wasn't creepy at all. I'd been imagining a dim room full of ancient dusty bottles and echoing walls, but in fact, the earl's cellar was very modern. The red brick walls and old stone floor were lit up with soft, warm light, and two rows of vaults housed countless bottles, all neatly stacked on top of one another like they contained messages and were waiting to be shipped out to sea.

At the far end was an enormous stack of wine crates with the names of suppliers stamped on the sides. I walked along the vaults, enjoying the cool air on my skin, scouring the bottles for the telltale gold foil top. My eyes widened as I took in all the names of the wines, from Barolo and Châteauneuf-du-Pape to zinfandel. The earl's wine collection covered countless countries, grapes, and producers. Had he known how all these wines tasted? Could anyone?

My eyes finally found the champagne section, and I could see the space where several bottles had been lifted from their home. "This must be the right champagne," I said into the echoey room, hoping that perhaps a friendly cellar ghost might appear and help me. I waited, but nothing. So much for help from the spirit world. I grabbed an empty wine crate and carefully retrieved six bottles, trying not to shudder as I considered what each one cost and how easy they were to drop and shatter.

I made my way back to the kitchen, holding the crate as if it were a newborn baby, and walking as quickly as I dared.

"Pops!"

I blinked a few times, but yes, there was Florence and with her were Gaurav and Hamish, all standing around the kitchen table. Hamish was helping Belinda lift a giant vat of creamy scrambled eggs and coax its contents into the elegant silver platters.

"We were walking back when we overheard one of the huntsmen saying the breakfast was going ahead," Gaurav explained.

"So naturally, we came to lend a hand," Florence said. "And take our minds off the show tomorrow," she added in a quieter voice.

I laughed in surprise. Were the bakers really that desperate to forget about the competition they'd offer their services as cooks?

"What a lovely bunch," Belinda said, her dark eyes flashing. "Now let's get cracking."

I read out the rest of Katie's schedule to the Broomewode staff as well as my motley crew of helpers, and somehow we managed to get crispy bacon, black pudding, pork and sage *and* Cumberland sausages, hash browns, and mounds of buttered toast onto platters. There were kippers, mushrooms, baked tomatoes, and some inscrutable dish for vegans.

Florence, glamorous as always, offered to help serve. I couldn't help but wonder if she just wanted an opportunity to flirt with some handsome, rich, and eligible hunters, but I could see how thankful Belinda was for the extra hands. Florence donned one of the white aprons the other servers wore and lifted a silver dish.

Hamish wiped the sweat from his brow and came to my side. "We thought some extra eyes inside Broomewode Hall, as well as hands, wouldn't go amiss, if you catch my drift."

Ahhh, clever Hamish. His detective senses were quivering as much as mine. Something about the earl's fall was off. What had he been doing before the hunt? How had he acted during it? No doubt everyone at the breakfast would be talking of nothing else.

"Perfect," I whispered back. Florence was made for the role of a beautiful spy, if only she didn't get distracted. "I'll join her." I took an apron and two jugs of freshly squeezed orange juice and prepared myself for my next role.

ollowing the line of servers, I weaved my way along the narrow corridor and up the servants' staircase to the main house. I suddenly felt nervous. I'd taken on many guises to get inside Broomewode Hall: fake reporter, cake deliverer, and now waitress. It all felt so at odds with going on a date with Benedict. But I was here to help him, I reminded myself. And part of that was investigating his father's sudden death. I had to keep my wits about me and not be intimidated by a room full of hungry hunters. I'd follow Florence's lead and be fine.

We entered the wide hall on the main floor and headed for the dining-room door. A huge part of me hoped that the painting of the old countess with my baby blanket pattern as her shawl had been returned to its position on the far right wall. It had been "taken out for cleaning" when I'd come to have a closer look and seemed to have been gone for weeks.

One of the kitchen staff halted at the door and turned to instruct the rest of us where the food needed to be placed.

"Set the platters in the spaces cleared and remember to work from the right."

"Work from the right?" I prodded Florence, confused.

"You serve to the right of the person in front of you," she whispered. "Just follow my lead."

The server flung open the door, and there was Tilbury, the butler, ready and waiting to announce in the most regal manner, "Breakfast is served."

The scene before me was one of pure opulence. The room was so different to the image I held in my mind. Yes, there were the enormous bay windows, framed by heavy tapestried curtains woven through with gold. The mahogany sideboards and display cabinets filled with china. The gorgeous cream wallpaper reaching up to the paneled ceilings, bordered by a deep red runner. But the antique dining table, previously empty save for a fancy pair of silver candelabra sticks, had been moved into the center of the room and was now full of splendid flower arrangements. Blooms of deep red were offset against vibrant green sprays, and despite it being afternoon, tall, tapered candles were lit in a row down the breadth of the table. Crystal of all shapes and sizes sat beside the loveliest china set I'd ever seen. The whole scene was beautiful, magical even, and my heart hurt for Benedict, how he wasn't going to be able to enjoy any of it, how it was all such a farce. The atmosphere was solemn, and the men talked in low voices. I didn't envy them: I'd no idea how I'd behave if I was asked to sit down for a grand breakfast that should have been hosted by a recently dead earl.

I waited to be told where to place my dish of triangle-shaped toasts and marveled at how elegantly and swiftly the other servers delivered their wares. Even Florence made the whole thing look glamorous, though I should have known she'd look every bit the pro. Waiting, I took the opportunity to look around the walls... No painting. In fact, where the old countess's portrait had been hanging was now an oil painting of the earl and his horse. I shuddered. What an ill-fated portrait. Had it been painted recently? I wondered if I should suggest taking it down but then figured that might only serve to draw more attention to it. The desire to throw a sheet over the thing was strong. I sighed. What had they done with the old painting? Surely it didn't take weeks to clean? Had the Champneys guessed that it was of special interest to me? But why should it matter, even if it was? I knew it was silly, but something in me felt incomplete knowing that the painting that had brought me to Broomewode in the first place had suddenly disappeared.

Beatrice and Tilbury were in charge of champagne, taking a bottle each from the silver ice buckets near the table and quietly popping the corks. They circled the hunters silently, everything was done in a swift motion, charging glasses so carefully, never a drop spilled or overflowed.

I stepped back and went to help Florence put out the little butter dishes.

"Do you see?" she said under her breath. "They're sharing photos from the day already. Look at them all—horse-mad and not a thought for the dearly departed."

I placed my butter dish down and prowled among the invited guests and saw that Florence was right. It seemed like everyone had camera phones with them and had started snapping right from the beginning of the meet, horses with their heads held high, the riders posed with arms either side of their hips. All the deep colors popped on the crystal-clear viewfinders, the rolling hills vivid green and the hunt always in motion. I caught Florence looking, too—though she was more likely imagining herself in a flowing gown astride a muscular horse for an Italian *Vogue* shoot than admiring the composition.

Beatrice called me over and asked if I'd circulate with a silver pot of coffee. I nodded, looking at the silky black liquid longingly—it had been far too long since my last fix. Maybe I could sneak one in the kitchen after my duties were done.

I walked around the table, doing my best to melt into the background just like the other servers, when I couldn't help but notice one older hunter talking loudly about a farmer. Could it be the farmer whose tractor nearly killed me? I had to find out.

I went to top up his barely touched coffee cup and sneaked a look at the photos he was sharing with his neighbor. The two men were laughing deep belly laughs, and as I leaned over I saw it was Farmer Riley and they were looking at photos of him red in the face.

"He was shaking his fist at the earl, the fool, like His Lordship cared a wink," the man holding the camera said.

The other one guffawed. "When is Riley going to understand that the earl can do what he wants? It's his land, after all. If he wants the hunt to go through it, then so it shall pass."

"May he rest in peace," the other man said hastily.

There was a moment of silence before the other man said, "Indeed," and then, "It was jolly funny when the earl simply jumped the fence and the rest of us followed. He had spirit."

"That he did."

I stepped away. So the farmer had tried to keep Robert Champney off of his land anyway, despite their previous fight and the earl disregarding his point of view. Was it possible, then, that Farmer Riley was so angry that he set a trap for the earl? If Robert Champney always returned early, and by the same route, to be on hand when the hunt returned for breakfast, could an annoyed and vengeful farmer have set a trap to knock the returning earl off his horse? Perhaps he'd only planned for the rider to take a humiliating fall, but the prank had gone horribly, horribly wrong. I felt cold at the thought.

I wanted to tell Hamish what I'd seen, but Charles Radlier, the Master of the hunt, was waving to get my attention. I glanced down at my apron. He obviously thought I worked for the Hall.

"Excuse me, miss," he said in a grand voice, "I was wondering what we might be able to rustle up for something to toast the earl with. I want to say a few words about Robert Champney and drink a toast to him. But champagne is too festive. Can you suggest something else?"

I stared at him. I had zero clue about what to toast with. What did you drink to salute the recently departed?

He looked at me expectantly. Despite his composure and good manners, the man was obviously shaken up. I guessed it was a British thing—just keep calm and carry on.

"I'll find out," I replied.

He thanked me and returned to his seat. The men were obviously enjoying the good food and drink, and the melancholy mood was shifting.

I told Florence I'd be back in a minute and quickly made my way to the kitchen, where Beatrice had returned to fetch more English mustard. She'd know what to do.

But when I'd snaked back down the narrow servants'

corridors, I found Benedict in the kitchen, drinking a glass of water by the sink, staring out of the window.

I approached him and placed a hand on his lower back. He turned, surprised, but smiled when he saw me, his warm eyes crinkling at the corners.

"How are you holding up?" I asked, knowing that it was probably a stupid question.

"I'm okay. It's all so surreal. I don't think I've quite got my head around the fact that my father's dead."

I told him it was to be expected—there were so many layers to grief.

"The police are here," he said, gesturing at the window.

I glanced out and recognized two familiar figures. DI Hembly and Sergeant Lane were talking to some of the staff. I could see Trim, the reporter, trying to muscle in on the action. What a story he'd have. No doubt he could scoop the bigger papers or perhaps sell them the story, as he was first on the scene. I told Benedict about the Master of the hunt's suggestion, and he replied that his father had a favorite burgundy. "It would be a nice gesture to raise a toast with a bottle. I'll show you where it is—he kept it in a special vault."

Benedict was so decisive, in control. He was already stepping into the role of earl.

I followed him back down the flagstone stairs to the wine cellar.

Benedict told me about the earl's trip to Burgundy when he discovered the wine. "He was so thrilled with how sumptuous it was that he ordered every bottle they had in stock."

I raised my eyebrows.

Benedict shook his head. "My father could be a little over the top. He didn't exactly abide by the idea that less is more."

We entered the cool cellar, and Benedict went straight to a small vault in the corner.

"This shouldn't be open," Benedict murmured, and then I noticed that a door that led to another set of stairs was ajar.

"Where does that go?" I asked as Benedict clicked the door shut.

"It goes straight to the outside. We use it to bring up the wine for garden parties."

I handed Benedict an empty crate, and he carefully filled it with bottles of expensive-looking wine. The crate looked heavy.

"It must be difficult for Katie to carry the wine upstairs at her age," I said. "Why doesn't Tilbury do it?"

"He suffers from claustrophobia, so Katie always gets the wine."

As Benedict lifted the crate, I remembered Katie's careful schedule. She ran a tight ship—I wondered what had stopped her from collecting all the champagne.

Back in the kitchen, Benedict gave the wine to Tilbury to decant.

Tilbury didn't look best pleased to see me. I guess in his mind, I'd snooped around Broomewode Hall too many times not to be a suspicious character. It was a shame, because if I could somehow befriend Tilbury, I knew I'd get some insider gossip. As butler, he must be privy to everything that went on in this grand house. I'd observed how excellent he was at sneaking up on someone. His footsteps were freakishly quiet. But no, he ignored me completely and busied himself with the wine.

"Ah, there you are." Charles, the Master of the hunt, strode into the kitchen. Obviously, I'd taken too long to find something suitable for his toast. For Benedict's sake, I tried not to roll my eyes. I had to keep reminding myself that this was his world.

Benedict explained that the burgundy had been opened and needed to breathe for a few minutes before they could make the toast. Charles replied that it was a fine choice and that his father would be proud. I could tell Benedict was moved by his words, but the moment was shattered by a loud knocking at the staff door.

A voice called out "hello," and I recognized it as belonging to Trim. Was he seriously trying to push his way into the hunt breakfast?

It turned out that I wasn't the only one who knew who was at the door. "Don't worry," Charles said to Benedict. "I'll get rid of that reporter. He's been a pest all day."

Benedict thanked him, and for the first time, he appeared to be overwhelmed. I wanted to comfort him, but with Tilbury decanting the wine and Beatrice back to brew more coffee, any intimate words would have an audience I knew neither of us wanted.

"Time to go now. This is a private affair." Charles's voice echoed in the corridor, the note of annoyance apparent. Obviously Trim wasn't taking no for an answer, but he hadn't reckoned on the willfulness of the Master of the hunt. Within seconds, a loud slam let us know that Charles had simply shut the door on Trim. I felt bad for the guy (I knew what it was like to place truth at the center of everything, to want *answers*), but interrupting a breakfast turned wake wasn't the best way to go about it.

Charles returned and asked Tilbury and Beatrice to carry

the decanters full of the rich red wine back to the dining room.

Benedict said he'd join them in a minute and turned to me. "Poppy, about this evening..."

Of course, he'd postpone our date. I'd expected that. But now I wondered if he'd cancel altogether, now that he was the Earl of Frome. I waited, somewhat anxiously, to see which way he'd play it, but whatever he was going to say was cut short by the arrival of the countess and Katie. They walked arm in arm, as if the countess couldn't stay upright without aid. She had changed out of her riding clothes and was wearing a loose black top tucked into smart black slacks with perfect creases down the middle. I didn't know how she managed to look so chic while in the throes of her grief.

"Benedict, darling," she said, coming to embrace her son. "I simply couldn't stay in my room. I must do something. Anything. I must ensure that the memory of your father is honored."

Again, I was kind of bemused as to how the countess spoke about her husband as if he were the king of England. "Naturally, he'll lie in state in the family chapel, where he can be visited and due respects be paid." Her voice wobbled. "And then there's the funeral to arrange."

I was pretty sure that the police would be taking the body, but I kept quiet. The countess was formidable. She turned to Katie and asked her to supervise giving the chapel a good clean. "And flowers. I must phone the florist immediately."

Wow, the countess really knew how to go from treating Katie as if she were her beloved friend to servant. But Katie appeared used to this sudden switch and dutifully replied that she'd get on to cleaning the chapel straightaway. "I'll take

Sally," she said. "She's got better knees than me and can get into the corners."

Katie left, and the countess said, "I'm going to make sure that pesky reporter has left. What appalling manners."

Benedict assured her the reporter had been shooed off already, so she tottered off to phone the florist.

Benedict and I were alone again. "Poppy, what I was trying to say earlier is that I'm so sorry that I'll have to cancel our date this evening."

"Of course!" I said, surprised by the apology. Was he going to tell me he couldn't see me at all now that he was the lord of the manor?

Benedict took my hands. My heart thumped in my chest. His cheeks flushed, and he blinked at me sweetly. My breath caught. An accumulation of small vibrations flooded my body. I was tingling. I realized I wanted him to kiss me. Was he going to kiss me? I felt my eyelashes flutter closed.

But an unpleasantly loud throat clearing caused my eyes to snap back open.

It was the countess. *Cringe.* Had she just witnessed that moment of tenderness between me and her son? I wanted the floor to open up and swallow me whole.

In a quiet, tight voice, she said, "Obviously, now my son's the earl, he'll be dating women of his class. I'm sure you understand, dear." And with that shocker of a statement, she swept out of the room.

I watched her black silhouette disappear into the hallway. I felt such shame as I'd never known before. A woman of his class? What was this, the 1800s? And then the shame was swiftly replaced by anger. How dare she!

Benedict looked appalled. "I'm so sorry. My mother's

obviously still in shock. Please pay her no attention. Let's erase that awful moment."

But I couldn't halt the sinking feeling in the pit of my stomach. Benedict was destined to end up with someone fancy and titled—just like his ex-girlfriend Lady Ophelia Wren. What was I thinking? Maybe I should back away now before I got really hurt.

"Poppy," Benedict said softly, "where have you gone inside that lovely head of yours?"

I realized I'd been staring at the ground and raised my eyes to meet his. "I..."

But the countess called out her son's name and asked him to go to his father's study to call the family solicitor immediately. The tone of her voice had changed again, and she sounded scared.

"Go," I said. "We can talk later."

Benedict nodded grimly.

I stood in the kitchen, my mind ablaze. I didn't know where to put myself. I'd agreed to help at the breakfast for Benedict's sake, but his mother had made it quite clear not only was I not necessary, I also wasn't wanted. Well, at least I'd managed to snoop a little. The oil painting of the old countess was gone, and the farmer and the earl had clearly gotten into it today. I decided enough was enough for one morning. I'd collect Hamish, Gaurav, and Florence and head back to the inn.

Mind made up, I was on my way to the dining hall when Benedict appeared again. He looked sick.

"What is it?" I asked, fear growing.

He didn't speak, just handed me two pieces of paper. They were two handwritten notes.

You think you'll get away with it, but you won't. I'll get my own back. You've been warned.

You are an evil man and evil is always punished.

"My God," I said. I recognized the handwriting from the schedule. It was Katie's.

CHAPTER 13

I had to wait until breakfast was over to collect the other contestants. The countess had called Benedict away again. For now, he was set to speak to the police, who were still roaming the grounds around Broomewode Hall.

Katie's handwriting was unmistakable, looping and girlish—so at odds with the threatening words it spelled out. It didn't add up. Yet there was no doubt it belonged to her. My head was spinning. Sweet Katie Donegal, who offered her arms to the countess in comfort, who stayed by her side as she grieved? Katie, who worked herself to the bone for the family, running the kitchen, organizing events, and doing much more in between. She was more than just a staff member. What possible reason could she have to threaten the earl?

Florence linked her arm through mine as we made our way back to the inn, chatting merrily about the hunters. But Hamish was more attuned to how I was feeling. When Florence stopped for air, he simply asked, "What happened?"

and then I told the three of them that Benedict had found some threatening notes left in his father's study.

"I recognized the handwriting," I said. But so much of me didn't want to believe that Katie had written those notes, I didn't say anything further. "They're probably with the police now."

Hamish raised a brow.

"Let's talk about it later," I said quietly. I needed more time to think.

Back at the inn, I realized I was famished. I'd helped serve an almighty feast to a bunch of hungry hunters, and now it was five p.m. and the effects of Ruta's roast chicken sandwich had long worn off.

I stuck my head into the kitchen and found Ruta and Pavel cleaning up and looking exhausted but pleased with themselves. "What a crazy day," Ruta said. "I'm very sorry about the earl, but business was roaring all afternoon. Everyone who couldn't find an excuse to be up at the Hall was here gossiping or raising a glass to His Lordship." She chuckled. "I got the feeling when I arrived here that he wasn't well-liked, but like so many unpleasant things, he improved in memory."

I wondered if the countess's rudeness to me would improve in memory and doubted it very much. I'd discovered that when I was upset, baking helped ease my mind. As the chef and her assistant prepared for the dinner crowd, I asked if I could bake some madeleines for the baking show contestants. Ruta looked at me like it was an odd request but, after a glance at my face, gave me the go-ahead. Despite the drama of the day, simple things like baking and serving my friends something delicious and comforting after a difficult time felt like a real privilege. I set the oven temperature, poured the mix into a madeleine tin with sixteen individual slots and set the timer. It was nice to listen passively as Ruta and Pavel chattered away.

When the timer dinged, I took the madeleines from the oven, popped them from their silicone cases, arranged the warm cakes on a round dish and took them over to the bakers' table, where a cafetière of coffee was making the rounds. As much as I needed my caffeine fix, part of me ached for something stronger. I shuddered, remembering the countess's cruel words, Katie's note, and the earl's lifeless body, but was determined to put the whole sorry mess out of my mind for at least the next half hour.

There were some seriously satisfying oohs and ahhs as I set the madeleines down, and each of the bakers grabbed two each, scoffing them down hungrily. Florence was the first to reach for more.

"I'm so glad you're out of the competition, Poppy, or you'd win for sure," she said. "These are delicious."

I was pleased with her praise though suspected she was very glad to have me out of the competition along with every other baker she'd triumphed over. "Today was so stressful," she said, widening her eyes. "And now we've got to think about tomorrow's bake."

Gaurav groaned. "With everything this afternoon, I'd almost managed to put the competition out of my mind. My nerves are shot through."

The group talked about their chocolate exploits, and I munched on madeleines, happy to let their chatter wash over me. My mind couldn't focus on any one thing. It kept flitting from the earl to Katie, from the countess to Benedict, from the photo of my mother, Valerie. Valerie. I pulled out my phone and hopelessly hit dial on Joanna's number, knowing there'd be no answer but wanting to try nonetheless. This time I was informed that the person I was trying to reach had a full mailbox. I was invited to try again later. I fought the urge to throw my phone against the wall.

"You okay, Pops?" Hamish asked, pointing at my phone, which I gripped as though it were an enemy. I didn't know what to say, where to start.

The cafetière was empty, and I volunteered to get a refill.

Eve was busy, so I slipped behind the bar, washing away the soggy brown grains, drying the glass and spooning more aromatic ground coffee into its depths. When I turned to add hot water from the coffee machine, I was surprised to see Florence standing at the bar. She told me that she wanted to talk to me privately. I was puzzled but encouraged her to continue with a nod of my head.

"I know it's been a seriously long day already, but I was still counting on some happy eggs tomorrow to make my signature bake sing." She paused, and I watched in wonder as Florence subtly arranged her features into a more innocent expression. "I was wondering if you could make sure that it's only me who gets the 'happy' eggs."

"What do you mean?" I asked. Surely, she wasn't asking for some favoritism here? Susan's eggs were available to anybody who wanted to purchase them. "I told all three of you I'd pick up some more eggs from Susan in the morning. The hunt took all the eggs the farm had in stock."

Florence knitted her fingers as she talked. "I can see you're thinking badly of me, Pops. Please don't. It's just that I need to win more than the others."

"Oh, Florence. *Everyone* wants to win."

"No, you don't understand. It's more than that. My agent says if I win, he could work on a TV deal for me. But no one wants to watch a cooking show hosted by a runner-up."

I shook my head. I had always suspected Florence of being selfish, but it seemed she'd happily cut corners and sneak around to win. I told her it was up to Susan who she sold her eggs to, not me, and swiftly changed the subject by handing her the now full cafetière. Florence and I had a good friendship, but I had no intention of choosing sides. I wished they could all win.

I was about to tell Florence to go back to the table when an electric charge coursed through my body. I startled, jolted with surprise. I wasn't touching anyone. Where had that come from?

I looked around the pub and then saw Elspeth Peach and Jonathon Pine emerge from the doorway. The two witches made me hum like a tuning fork.

As usual, Elspeth looked immaculate in a cream silk shirt, single strand of pearls, and white hair pulled back into a sleek ponytail. Jonathon was his usual cool self, trademark blue shirt matching his blue eyes, dark jeans. But today his face lacked his usual sparkle, and there was worry in Elspeth's expression, too.

"We're so glad to see you in one piece," Elspeth said softly, taking my warm hands in her cool ones and squeezing tight. I felt the buzz of connection. I'd never get used to the balance of electricity with serenity that always came with an embrace from Elspeth.

I assured her that I was okay, that I'd been nowhere near the earl when he died but present at the scene afterwards.

"Nothing's adding up. My body might be fine, but my mind is a whirl."

"Two accidents in the same number of days," Jonathon said. I could almost hear the words he couldn't say out loud: *The electric field in Broomewode is troubled. Something's wrong.*

"They won't cancel the filming, will they?" Florence asked. "Because of the earl's death?"

I'd almost forgotten Florence was still standing there. I turned to look at her. She was pale, stricken at the idea that the competition might not go ahead this weekend.

"No, no," Jonathon said. "It won't come to that. The production company have spoken with the countess, but she insisted that the filming continue. She was certain it's what the late earl would have wanted."

"Ah, I see," Florence said, relief washing across her face.

But I didn't see. I didn't see at all. How was she so sure what the earl would have wanted? Wasn't it more a case of what the countess wanted? I knew that the money from the film company was vital to Broomewode Hall. It was a hard fact I'd learned my first week in the village.

"We can't stay," Elspeth said, sorrow in her eyes. "But please keep yourself safe. Both of you," she continued, looking first at Florence and then at me. More quietly, she added, "Remember what I've taught you."

"We have to go," Jonathon said, still solemn. "I recommend both of you get an early night. Sleep well and keep safe."

THE REST of the night passed in a blur. I didn't want to be alone, so I joined the bakers for dinner in the next village. At Florence's behest, we dined at a tapas restaurant one of her London friends had recommended. Getting out of Broomewode had seemed like a good idea, so I'd accepted the invitation. I should have been on a date with Benedict, and instead I was dining with several very nervous baking contestants, but it was so much better than sitting home wondering what might have been. I didn't think there would be a rescheduling of our date. The Countess of Frome had been very clear that the new earl couldn't slum it with the likes of me. Sheesh. I hadn't realized how much I was looking forward to dinner with Benedict until there was no hope of it taking place.

Gaurav had driven down from Birmingham this week, and he drove us in his Citroen hatchback. We chattered and laughed, talked about chocolate recipes, but not one of them would tell me what they were planning to make for the showstopper. No amount of needling and whining from me made a difference. The remaining three bakers were as superstitious as anything. I couldn't believe it! Usually they couldn't wait to tell me what they'd spent the week dreaming up and practicing. Now I couldn't even get a hint. So I left them to their secrecy—after all, being annoyed that they kept secrets from me was too much like the pot calling the witch black. Instead, I enjoyed the food—oozing onion and potato tortilla, salty Padrón peppers, squid ink, and saffron risotto, and fine, delicate slices of Iberian ham, which melted on my tongue. We finished the lot off with slices of almond torte.

Gaurav ferried us back to the inn, and the three finalists headed straight upstairs to get their rest.

It was a lovely evening, but it wasn't the one I'd planned. I thought of my new red dress still hanging in my wardrobe at home, the earrings snug in their fabric pocket. Benedict. My heart beat double quick at the thought, and yet my stomach dropped at the same time. Where would he have taken me this evening? What would we have talked about? How would the night have ended? I glanced up toward Broomewode Hall, wondering what was going on up there.

I shook my head. There was no use indulging what-ifs. But I knew I couldn't sleep.

I headed to the bar, where Eve was polishing glasses, a long shift finally over, the new girl taking over to serve the few customers left and close. The kitchen was long shut. It was strange to see the pub so empty after such a busy day. Eve smiled a tired smile and invited me to join her in a nightcap.

"I've been waiting to talk all evening," Eve said, pouring us both a generous glass of Malbec. "Elspeth is worried. I'm worried. Susan, too."

I forced a small laugh. "Do you all have a worry hotline I don't know about?"

Eve smiled, sadness creeping in with the tiredness now. "The tragedy, it's hit us hard. Especially Susan. She was close to the earl, or at least her late husband was."

"Of course," I said. I'd forgotten that Susan and her late husband had moved here because of the close friendship between her husband and Robert Champney, the Earl of Frome. Poor Susan.

"I heard the countess sobbed and begged the police to let her husband lie in peace in the family chapel, though the police took the body away, of course. Apparently, she still made Katie and one of the maids clean the chapel all afternoon."

"Katie's been busy," I said somewhat dryly. I thought of those threatening notes she'd left the earl. I couldn't understand how she could act like the faithful servant while she'd been sending such horrible messages. Could there be a link to the earl's death?

I was struck with the desire to tell Eve about the notes and see what she could make of them. Maybe she knew why the Broomewode cook had it in for the earl, but an instinct stopped me. I was still exploring my witch powers, but I'd learned to listen to my instincts. Mostly. I'd left Benedict examining the notes. No doubt he'd now passed them on to the police.

However, Robert Champney's death wasn't the only mystery currently bothering me. I wanted to see if Eve could help me with the mystery of Joanna. I realized I hadn't had a chance to really tell her about my encounter. I'd been too stunned the day of the accident. I told Eve everything and explained how I still couldn't get hold of the woman I'd had coffee with and who'd saved my life and been injured in the process.

"I didn't know Joanna was coming for a visit, either," Eve said. "Mavis always gets very excited when she's coming. Even though she doesn't live far away, she's busy with her work, so it's always a treat when she comes, and Mavis isn't shy about letting the world know her business."

"Is there anything you could tell me about Joanna? Something that might help me understand why she bolted yesterday?"

But Eve just shook her head. "Not especially. It seems very odd behavior. Joanna seems like a sensible woman, not one to run off with a bleeding head."

Yet that was exactly what she did. I sighed. I felt further from the truth than ever.

"One minute she was there," I explained, "and then the next, *poof!* Just a flash of blond hair and then she vanished."

Eve looked puzzled. "Blond hair?"

I nodded. "Joanna has a choppy blond bob."

Eve's forehead crinkled further. "She's always been a redhead. Must have dyed it, though I can't imagine her as a blond."

"You're kidding. Could she have dyed her hair recently?"

Eve shrugged. "Maybe. But she's always been very proud of being a 'ginger,' and she always said she'd never cut her long hair."

"Is she"—I glanced around to make sure no one could overhear me—"one of us?"

Eve stared. "You mean a witch?"

I nodded.

"No. She's utterly practical and earthbound."

I was getting a very strange feeling about "Joanna."

If Joanna hadn't dyed her hair, then who was the woman I met?

CHAPTER 14

*T*he next morning, I arrived at work already exhausted. The idea of sleep had slipped through my fingers as I tossed and turned, trying to remember every detail of meeting Joanna. Were there red roots showing in her hair? Any other telltale sides of it being dyed? Did she bear a resemblance to Mavis at the newspaper?

I'd been so keyed up meeting her, and then the tractor hit and completely derailed our visit. If only I'd paid more attention to the small things, but I was too caught up in my own excitement. I'd been anticipating our meeting all week, going through the questions I wanted to ask her about Valerie—her likes and dislikes, any memories of that summer before I was born, and most importantly who she'd dated. Joanna had told me she thought Valerie had gone to Glasgow, but now I was having doubts. The more I thought about it, the more the Joanna I met seemed like an imposter. Which seemed absurd. But, as Gerry had reminded me, there was something odd about Broomewode. Sometimes it was hard not to feel like I was at the center of a big conspiracy.

But if my hunch was right, and it wasn't Joanna at all, then who did I meet? Why the instant chemical buzz when I saw her? And what did she have to gain by pretending to be Joanna?

I'd called the number for Joanna so many times that my fingertips pressed the buttons almost by themselves. The phone was still out of service. But today I was determined to find where she was and who she was. I'd stop at nothing to get to the bottom of this. My first port of call was to find out Joanna's address and drive to her home.

In the meantime, I had to get on with work at the inn.

If Ruta noticed the blue shadows beneath my eyes, she had the courtesy not to mention it. I kept my head down and tried to remember the love of baking that had brought me to the inn in the first place, easing myself into a gentle rhythm: measure, sieve, stir, mix. Pour, fold, smooth. It was early on Saturday morning. Though the inn wouldn't be as busy as yesterday, there were still hungry mouths to feed and sweet tooths to satisfy. I couldn't slack off on my day job.

I wondered if the baking contest semifinalists had slept well and doubted it. Which reminded me they all wanted some of Susan's special eggs. I texted her and was relieved when she said she had eggs for all the contestants and she'd bring them down to the inn herself.

Soon it was time to lay out the breakfast buffet. I took my basket of apple muffins to the table and caught sight of Hamish and Gaurav quietly sipping coffee in the corner. They weren't speaking; Hamish's gaze was trained out of the window, a whimsical look on his face. I wondered if his coping mechanism was to imagine being somewhere else entirely. A beach in Antigua, a tavern in the Alps eating fondue? Or maybe just at home in the Highlands with his Shetland ponies. Gaurav, on the other hand, was intensely focused. It was as if he were running recipes through his mind like a data sample. No sign of Florence yet, of course. She was surely perfecting her makeup, teasing her hair into a style that looked effortless yet took hours.

I arranged the basket and then took two muffins over to the men.

They smiled as I approached, but the pre-filming tension was thicker than the butter we served from the neighboring dairy farm. If only I could reassure them; there was truly nothing else they could do at this point—just go in and do their best.

I presented the muffins like I was giving them an award. If only I could crown them both winners!

They thanked me, and I told them that I would slip away during my break and give them moral support in the visitors' area as soon as I could.

"Any luck with the happy eggs?" Hamish asked.

"Susan just texted. She'll be here in a moment with enough for all of you."

"Ah, an egg angel," Gaurav said. "Just what the baking gods ordered today."

I tried to make small talk to ease both bakers' nerves, but I was met with monosyllabic mutterings. I didn't take it personally, but it was a relief when Susan arrived carrying a heavy-looking basket.

She looked flustered, and I realized she'd be on her way to the morning market. It was very kind of her to deliver the eggs for the contest. I never would have made it to the farm and back in time.

But Susan was a good saleswoman, and if she felt hurried, she didn't let on. "Morning, all," she said, her warm voice booming. "Jolly lovely day for a spot of baking. And the market. Lots of people will be out." She lifted the basket onto the table and brought out three cartons of eggs. "Now these eggs come from very happy hens. It's what makes their yolks so orange and creamy. They might look smaller than you're used to, but that's because they're mighty." She glanced at the two men. "I'm happy to give you the eggs and wish you all the luck in the world. If you happened to mention my eggs on camera, that would be wonderful."

Gaurav and Hamish both lit up and thanked her profusely. They promised they'd try to slip in a word about her eggs when they were interviewed as they were baking today. I knew those eggs would stand them in good stead for the competition. Susan had no idea what a gift her produce was, even if it was only the psychological lift of knowing the eggs were from happy hens. She chuckled. "If only everyone was as grateful as you chaps."

There was a loud throat clear, and everyone turned to see Florence, glaring. She looked, well, astonishing. She'd obviously been saving her best outfit for the semifinals. If she made it through this weekend, then goodness knows how she'd top this. She was wearing a ruby-red cotton dress with a sweetheart neckline, the straps wide and fastened with a dramatic bow. The soft fabric skimmed her calves. Her feet were encased in buttery-looking black leather ballet pumps. And the hair: curled and piled high in a ponytail to cascade down her back, waterfall-style. Her lipstick was a complementary shade of cherry and her eyes lined with feline flicks. But her beauty was marred by her expression.

"Don't worry, Florence," Susan said quickly. "I've got yours, too. And might I add that you look delectable."

I knew that Florence didn't think Susan had forgotten her. She was livid with me that all the bakers now had Susan's eggs. *Well, sorry, Florence, but not sorry. I never intended to choose sides.*

"Good luck, my dears," Susan said, wishing them well before she left for the market.

I told Florence her outfit was fabulous, but her glare didn't drop. Oh well. She'd soon forget all about me and the eggs the second camera lights turned green.

I wished them all good luck. "Break a leg," I added as they left the inn.

I returned to the kitchen to help Ruta and Pavel with the final parts of the breakfast spread. But when I staggered out under the weight of a silver platter of streaky bacon, I saw the detectives were lingering by the table the bakers had just vacated. I'd been expecting them to turn up—there were too many unknowns about the earl's death, and there were the threatening notes thrown into the mix. I put the bacon in its rightful place next to the sausages, smoothed down my hair, and tried not to feel nervous as Sgt. Lane waved me over.

He looked handsome as usual with his swept-back brown hair and those dimples. Perhaps even more handsome. Was it a tan? Yes—and a smattering of freckles.

"Poppy," he said, extending a hand to shake, "we've been looking for you."

So not what a girl wants to hear. The police looking for me?

"No need to look worried," he said, his smile deepening. "Just routine questions about what you saw yesterday."

DI Hembly nodded and shook my hand with a vigorous grip. "Do you have a moment?"

I agreed (of course) and prepared myself to be more grilled than the breakfast sausages.

"As you know, yesterday's tragedy has rippled through the village, and we need to get to the bottom of what happened."

Rippled through the village? Was DI Hembly getting poetic now?

"We need you to go through your movements step by step," he continued.

I took a breath and began. Since my mind had been running through the details of the last forty-eight hours, it was easy for me to recite the details of the day. I began with my early morning at the inn, my walk to the meet, talking with Oliver the horse breeder, and seeing the hunt depart. I'd returned to the inn for the rush and walked back again with the bakers, and shortly after our arrival, we'd heard the countess scream and I'd run with Hamish to where the earl had taken a fall.

As usual, Sgt. Lane took notes while DI Hembly asked questions and listened intently to my answers.

I continued my rundown of those horrible moments, the earl's lifeless body, Hamish spotting the missing button and Gaurav finding it. Then sharing Benedict's terrible slow walk back to the manor house.

"And when you approached the house, from which entrance did Katie Donegal emerge?"

"Oh," I said, startled. What a left-field question.

I closed my eyes for a moment. "It was the servants' entrance door."

"And the time?"

"The time," I repeated. I was getting a bad feeling about this. "Are you thinking this wasn't an accident?"

DI Hembly said, "There was a mark across Robert Champney's chest, about the height of the missing button."

"We believe a line of some sort was stretched across the path," Sgt. Lane continued. "And it knocked the earl from his horse."

"You mean?"

"Most likely," DI Hembly said solemnly. "Robert Champney was murdered."

I felt a shiver of horror run over me. "But why? Who would do such a thing?"

"That's what we're here to find out. You don't miss much. Did you notice any animosity lately? Did it seem like Robert Champney had any enemies?"

"Not enemies, per se," I said, inwardly glowing a little from the detective's compliment about my observation skills. "But he certainly wasn't very well liked in the neighborhood. He put on such airs and graces. It didn't win him the popularity vote. But surely that couldn't be enough of a reason to kill him."

"Hmm," Sgt. Lane murmured. "You saw the threatening notes Benedict Champney found in his father's study."

Sergeant Lane flipped back in his notebook and then read out what the terrible notes had said. "*You think you'll get away with it, but you won't. I'll get my own back. You've been warned.* And, *You are an evil man and evil is always punished.*"

"So he does have an enemy," DI Hembly said, leaning forward.

"I recognized the handwriting from the breakfast schedule. And it doesn't make sense."

"Who did the handwriting belong to, Miss Wilkinson?" DI Hembly asked.

I hated to say the words. "It belonged to Katie Donegal."

I realized I was holding in my stomach muscles, tensing like I was expecting a punch to the gut. But there was nothing. No response from either detective. Just more note-taking. Benedict would have told them it was Katie's handwriting. All I'd done was corroborate what they already knew, but I still felt terrible for bringing trouble to Katie. Though it did seem like she'd brought trouble on herself. And the earl.

Sweat was gathering at the nape of my neck, but I felt cold. Cold all the way inside.

I wanted to tell the detectives I didn't believe that Katie would hurt a fly. That she acted strangely sometimes, especially around Mitty, but she wasn't cruel. I knew in my *bones* she wasn't cruel. But before I could defend Katie, Trim strode into the pub. He was straight-backed, chest puffed up, and clutching a brown manila envelope.

"Detectives," he said, retucking his white shirt into his trousers. "I've been looking for you."

"We're in the middle of—" Sgt. Lane began, but Trim cut him off.

"I thought you'd like to see these." He handed DI Hembly the envelope. "I've printed off photos from the hunt. Thought they might be useful."

He stood, expectant as a schoolboy in front of a headmaster waiting for praise. I figured he was hoping they might give him some info in exchange. *Good luck with that, Trim.*

DI Hembly laid out the photos on the table, and Trim took that as an invitation to pull up a seat.

And then another uninvited guest appeared. Gerry. I

dipped my head in acknowledgment as he hovered, cross-legged genie-style, over the table. "Interesting," he mused. "Very interesting. Now that, that doesn't look good."

I followed Gerry's flickering pointing finger. There was a glossy photograph of the earl and the Master of the hunt, clearly having words, both of the men on horseback.

Sgt. Lane was also studying the same photo. "Do you know what was happening there?"

Trim replied that he'd heard a rumor that the earl was angry with the Master as he thought he was taking in a lot more money from the hunt club that had raised it to support the hunt than the earl was getting.

By now I could read the facial cues of both detectives, and the small look they exchanged confirmed that their next stop was to talk to the Master.

But Trim wasn't quite ready to let them go. He glanced at me and then asked them if they thought there was any connection between the earl's death and the tractor accident the day before.

"Why would you think that?" DI Hembly asked. He was the master at answering a question with a question. Such a cop.

"Well, Poppy here was almost killed by that wayward tractor, and the farmer was so riled up after his argument with the earl—"

"You were almost killed?" Sgt. Lane interrupted, turning to me.

I didn't know what to say. Yes, it was a little touch and go. I mean, no one could face a charging tractor and not fear for their life, but Joanna, or whoever she was, had saved me. "It was a freak accident," I said and explained in a roundabout way what had happened. I could have killed Trim, though. The last thing I wanted was to draw even more attention to myself. Luckily, neither detective asked me what I was doing at The Hourglass café in the first place. And then I scolded myself for being reticent. It wasn't illegal to meet someone for coffee.

"What's that tenant farmer's name?" DI Hembly asked Sgt. Lane, a deep line forming across his forehead.

Both Trim and the sergeant answered at the same time. "Nathaniel Riley."

"Right. He's on our list to speak to. Perhaps we should see him next."

"You don't think a freak accident has anything to do with the earl getting killed, do you?" I didn't really expect them to answer. I was mainly verbalizing my thoughts. Could there be a connection?

Trim answered me. "I was at the scene shortly after the tractor smashed into the café. Farmer Riley was there. He kept insisting he'd never leave his tractor in an unsafe manner." He paused, enjoying the intrigue.

"Do go on," Sgt. Lane said. He shot me a look of concern, and I raised my brows, silently telling him I was okay.

"Flirt," Gerry whispered.

I flinched. I'd almost forgotten he was floating beside me. Luckily, the sergeant was back to taking notes and hadn't seen me jump as though someone had stuck a pin in my arm.

Trim said, "Look, I'm not one to make trouble, but I've been in the pub many a time with Riley, and he *despised* the earl. Get a few drinks in him and he'd rant about how things needed to change and this jumped-up pretender had no right to order him about. That kind of thing. I hear the two of them had a huge fight Thursday. Apparently, he shouted at the earl and said he didn't want the hunt going through his property, as the horses trampled his crops, and last hunt they left the gates open and his sheep got out."

"That's true," I said, "at least about them having an argument. I drove past and saw the disagreement from afar."

"The earl wasn't going to take that—he shouted back, said it was his land and he could do what he liked with it. He reminded Riley that he was only a tenant. And that did *not* go down well."

I looked at Trim, unsure whether to be impressed by his sleuthing or embarrassed that he knew more than me. Seemed like Gerry felt the same. "I told you, Pops," he said. "There was more to that crash than you thought."

Trim glanced at DI Hembly. "And I'm sure you know that the earl owns The Hourglass café. The estate owns a number of businesses in the area."

Lane was scribbling in his notebook. Trim looked very pleased with himself. But my heart was in my sneakers. Could Farmer Riley have let the tractor crash into the coffee shop deliberately? If it was all a vendetta against the earl, then their dispute could have cost me my life.

CHAPTER 15

"**We**'ve certainly given them a lot to think about," Trim said when the detectives had left, presumably to visit Riley.

I frowned at Trim. "If you're right about the farmer, then that means he could have killed me trying to get his own back on the earl. Is he really that vindictive that he'd endanger innocent people? Some of the people in that café must be his neighbors."

"Told you, Pops," Gerry said. "Maybe everyone's right. Maybe you aren't safe in the village."

I glared at Gerry. But luckily Trim's gaze was turned downwards. "I don't know. I thought he was all bluster, just blowing off steam over a pint. Maybe if someone had reported him, we could have stopped this tragedy."

I wanted to say that without Joanna, the story could have been very different. But if it wasn't for Joanna, I would never have been at the café in the first place. Instead, I directed the attention away from me.

"I don't believe anyone would kill the earl. His scraps with the villagers were petty. Just minor disputes. Not something to inspire murder, surely."

Trim said he wouldn't be so sure. "I took photos of the crime scene people working the area." He got his camera and showed me a close-up shot of a tree. "This is where they think a rope or wire might have been attached."

I leaned in and examined the photo. Although it was subtle, there was definitely a groove in the bark—like a wire or rope would make if it was pulled taut. If a trap had been set for the earl, then this was a damning piece of evidence. I pictured the earl riding back to the hall, hurrying to keep his schedule. He wouldn't have even noticed a thin line stretched across the path until he struck it and it knocked him off his horse. It left a mark on the dead man's chest and explained how he'd lost a button. I shuddered to think of someone doing such a thing to the earl.

"Who would do such a thing?" I asked.

Gerry said, "Could have been any of them. All those horses and riders, people following on foot, and don't forget the anti-hunt types." I nodded, careful not to answer Gerry.

Trim took longer to answer. "I never thought much of Riley's nastiness, but he's an angry man, and he's been nursing his grievances against the earl for years. Maybe he simply snapped. When he tried to hurt the earl by destroying the café, his plan backfired and people blamed him for the accident. Maybe that drove him over the edge and he decided to finish the earl off with the very hunt they fought over."

I shuddered to think of that kind of hate building over the years, especially as I'd been in the path of that tractor, but Trim's theory definitely made a horrible kind of sense.

Trim headed back to the paper to work on his next front page.

I headed back to the kitchen to finish the morning shift. I worked quietly and quickly. As much as I loved my new job, there were so many pressing matters to follow up on. As soon as my shift was done, I had to keep my promise to the bakers. I'd make a stop at the competition tent and then get on the trail of the mysterious Joanna.

As the tent came into view, I couldn't believe next week was the last weekend of the show. The whole experience had gone by in a flash while I was participating, and it only seemed like a minute ago that I was the one sweating it out under the camera lights and trying not to crash and burn in front of millions of viewers.

I joined the group of visitors watching from behind the barrier, keeping silent as the cameras slid around, catching every tense moment. And the tension was palpable. I felt like I knew the people in the tent so well—the comic presenters, Jilly and Arty; the two judges, Elspeth and Jonathon; and the bakers who'd become my friends. The viewers at home followed the highs and lows, learned the unique talents of the presenters and bakers alike. But I had the inside track. I knew it took the team just three days to erect the baking tent, lay flooring, and install twelve workstations, each like a mini kitchen. I knew that every day, the ovens had to be tested. A sponge cake was slipped into their depths each morning before the bakers arrived to make sure everything was in order. Every time baking was placed into—or taken out of—

an oven, a cameraman had to follow. I could imagine, on a day like today, the last thing the bakers wanted was to grab a cameraman and tell them to watch their every move. Gaurav, the shyest of the three, must certainly find it a challenge. He was getting better at remaining composed when the judges and comedians interviewed him mid-flow. I suspected he'd be a viewer favorite as he overcame his shyness to explain his techniques. He was so very likable. But then, in their own way, they all were.

The weather played a huge part in how the day's baking went as well. The sun had come out to play most weekends. This made for glorious walks and a lovely light in the tent itself, but on hot summer days, baking here was a trial. Setting buttercream or whipping cream became trickier. The warm temperature today was going to pose problems for the bakers.

Since it was the penultimate weekend, the challenges were extra tough: They'd have to work with extreme speed, skill, and accuracy. On top of all that, working with chocolate needed the tent to be cool. From my viewing spot, I could see that Hamish was under pressure. He was whizzing around his workstation, trying to temper chocolate. I willed him to slow down or he'd overheat along with his chocolate. There were so many cameramen following each step. I cast my eye around for Elspeth and Jonathon, but they weren't in the tent. This was often the case. The judges weren't supposed to be there for the whole bake time in order to be more neutral when judging time arrived. They'd be resting in one of the side rooms of the tent, no doubt.

There was so much history to the tent; so many contestants had gone before these three, including me. I wondered if they felt the weight of past brilliant bakes bearing down, if they compared themselves to the ghosts of bakers past. It was such a special place. To my horror, I found myself welling up just thinking about it. *Enough, Pops. Enough.*

If Hamish was stressed, then Florence appeared to be the very epitome of serenity. Her dress, even more magnificent beneath the tent lights, swished and swayed as she stirred. Jilly was talking to her, though I couldn't catch what they were discussing. No doubt Florence was delivering a well-rehearsed piece about her chocolate Dobos torte. I stepped closer to listen, and she explained her approach to making the seven thin cake layers filled with chocolate buttercream and topped with caramel. It seemed like the one they had to make for the technical was coffee and walnut, each layer alternating between coffee buttercream and praline buttercream.

"And then there are the finely chopped nuts," Jilly said, eyebrow raised.

"Can't forget about the nuts," Florence agreed. "They go last, after covering the whole lot in chocolate ganache, apparently."

Florence was impressive. Even on the technical, where she had no idea what was in store or if she'd even recognize the bake, she managed to speak with authority and clarity.

She was also doing a grand job of keeping her dress clean. Even her apron was practically spotless. I didn't know how she managed it. I was forever spilling things down myself in the kitchen. A walking flour bomb twenty minutes into a shift. The second day of filming had always been a bit of a nightmare when I was on the show and had to show up in the same outfit as the day before. Florence would need to wear that dress again tomorrow for continuity, and she wouldn't risk spilling a drop of batter even if it meant working at a slightly slower pace than the others. Unless she had a second, identical dress in the closet at the inn. I wouldn't put it past her.

The rest of the crowd watched, enthralled, as the bakers were told they had thirty minutes left until they had to plate up. However, my eyes were drawn behind me, across the green field to where Sly was standing watching me, his ball at his feet, waiting to be thrown. I walked over, pretty sure he'd used his familiar magic to call me to him. He was such a clever dog. I bent down to retrieve the red ball, and Sly bounded up, his tongue hanging out, tail wagging in pleasure.

"Hello, boy," I whispered. "What are you doing here?" Rather than throwing his ball (I had visions of it flying across the tent's opening and landing in the middle of a bowl of melted chocolate), I stroked his soft coat. Sly rolled onto his back. The message was clear: *belly rubs, please.* And since I was depriving him of his favorite game, I obliged.

Laughing as he rolled around, I straightened and cast my eye around for his mom. But the smile soon dropped from my face as I spotted Susan. She was on the path that led to her farm, partly hidden by a tree, embroiled in what was clearly an intense conversation with Katie Donegal. The two were huddled together, so close, in fact, that I had to assume they were whispering. Something about their intensity suggested they weren't gossiping idly. I headed toward them. I had to know what those two were discussing.

Up close, Katie was ranting, red in the face and furious. A

shudder went through me as I overheard what she was so upset about.

"Why would the police think I would do such a thing? I feel so betrayed. It was Benedict or the countess who said such wicked things about me. Why would they? What reason could I possibly have to hurt the earl or the family? I've been loyal to that family all my working life."

I came up beside her, but Katie didn't even notice my arrival. She was whipping herself up into a frenzy, and Susan looked horrified.

"I've worked for the family for decades, and I've been a loyal, dedicated member of staff. I dare you to find anyone more faithful to the Champneys than me. I dare you!"

"I couldn't," Susan said quietly, her voice soft as silk. "Everything you're saying is true. You're a credit to the family. The earl himself used to say so to my late husband. And the countess relies on you so heavily. Why, you're like family to her."

But Katie was shaking her head vehemently, the color in her cheeks high.

I said Katie's name, trying to match Susan's soft tone. She turned, not looking delighted to see me. I said, "I believe everything you're saying, too, Katie. But..." I swallowed and took a deep breath, afraid of the reaction I might soon face. "I saw your notes myself. Benedict found them in the earl's study. It was the handwriting—it matched the schedule you gave me. And of course, Benedict recognized your hand-writing too."

"I didn't leave any notes!" she all but screamed.

I pretty much wanted to slink away from all the venom, not to mention the spittle flying out of her mouth, but I wouldn't figure out what happened to the earl by running away. As calmly as I could, and as well as I could remember, I repeated the content of those notes. "You're an evil man, and evil is always punished." I was pretty sure that was what one of them had said.

"Call the earl evil? I'd never!" Then she thought for a moment. "Wait. I did write to that useless butcher." She looked shaken. "I may have called him evil. I got a bit carried away with pen and paper when I was feeling particularly swindled."

I was trying to remember the other note. "There was something about 'I know what you've done and you won't get away with it.'"

Katie let out a little cry of frustration. "That was definitely intended for Derek, the butcher! I was sick and tired of his nonsense. He overcharges Broomewode Hall because he knows the earl won't allow me to buy meat anywhere else. Makes my blood boil."

"The butcher?" I said, and then I remembered Katie bad-mouthing Derek in Susan's barn.

"He's a swindler. Evil, if you ask me. But the earl would insist on using his meats, even though they were subpar."

Relief rushed through me. The butcher: It made perfect sense. "But how did the notes for Derek find themselves on the earl's desk?" Susan asked. "Do you think he saw them?"

Katie shrugged. I could see the despair setting in, replacing the rage that had consumed her moments ago. "I've no idea, luvvie. I've no idea. I certainly didn't put them there. Or into the police's hands."

"Maybe the butcher gave them to the earl, hoping to get you into trouble."

"Aye, he'd do that. Nasty little worm. He used to send me uncomplimentary messages too, you know."

I felt terrible. I knew Benedict had had no choice reporting those notes, but he'd landed Katie in deep waters, and now she was going under.

"Surely the police will believe you?" I said, desperate now to make amends. "Especially if other people can vouch for your ongoing feud with Derek?"

But Katie just shook her head sadly. "It doesn't matter who believes me now. I don't know what to do with myself. The countess has relieved me of my duties."

"What?" I echoed, shocked.

"No!" Susan gasped. "I don't believe it."

"She fired you?" I didn't care for the countess, but even for her, that was brutal.

Katie explained that the countess had told her that her services wouldn't be required until the police finished their investigation. Ever since the notes were discovered, she'd given poor Katie the cold shoulder.

"You should explain what happened," I said.

"It won't make any difference to her ladyship. I'm hurt to the quick, I am, and I'm not sticking around the manor house to watch other people swanning around my kitchen. I've worked myself to the bone for this place, and this is the thanks I get. I'm going to head into the village and enjoy a day off. It's just not right." She stomped off without saying goodbye.

Open-mouthed, Susan and I watched her leave.

"Poor Katie," Susan said, turning to me. "She doesn't know the half of it. The countess came over to the farmhouse late last night for tea and to talk. She didn't know what to do with herself with her husband taken so suddenly. She knew I'd been through the same thing and was seeking solace. All I could do was tell her how time is a healer, but when you're in the first throes of grief, it seems impossible that things will get better."

I nodded. Susan could be very sage. Maybe that was why she was so good at turning herbs into tonics—there was wisdom, as well as magic, in her fingers.

"The countess told me the earl had planned to fire Katie. She'd become increasingly belligerent and was spending so much time looking after Mitty that she was abandoning her duties to the family. If you ask me, she was glad to have an excuse to fire Katie."

"Whoa," I said. "After all those years of service? Surely the earl could see how important Mitty was to Katie and have a little compassion?"

"I'm afraid the earl wasn't the most compassionate of men," Susan said.

"Do you think Katie had an inkling she'd fallen out of favor?"

But Susan confessed she wasn't sure. The countess said Katie had received a verbal warning, but Katie denied this vehemently.

Susan grimaced, and I was certain my expression was the mirror image. If Katie knew that she was about to get fired, it made her story about the butcher less plausible. Her outrage might have been enough to write menacing notes, but was it enough for murder?

CHAPTER 16

I bid Susan and Sly a subdued goodbye and decided to make my way back to the inn. The bakers would be serving their bakes to Jonathon and Elspeth soon, and I didn't think I could stand to witness any more tension. I wanted all of them to win, and it was unbearable to watch them worry and know one of them would be sent home tomorrow.

Besides, I wanted to think. I couldn't believe that the countess would suspend Katie from her duties, but I could also see that in her eyes, the evidence was damning. It was Katie's handwriting. She didn't deny writing the notes, but if they were truly meant for the butcher, how could they have found their way to the earl's study?

I walked slowly, savoring the warm air, trying to take in the beauty of the rolling green fields. But not even the Somerset landscape could quell my sadness. Was no one in Broomewode who they appeared to be? Over the weeks, there had been so many false starts as I'd tried to find answers to where I'd come from. I found myself looking into the sky, at the puffs of cottony clouds, shielding my eyes against the sun, searching for the hawk. "Where are you?" I said into the blue. "Why can't you give me answers?" I laughed a little to myself then. Did I seriously think a bird of prey could sidle along-side me and tell me what was up? I shook my head, retied my ponytail, and told myself to get a grip.

But back at the inn, any notions of keeping a clear head disappeared as the first person I saw standing at the delivery entrance to the inn was Katie. An irate Katie, waving her arms about, red in the face. It was like she'd walked away from Susan and found another person to argue with. So much for a day off.

I stepped closer and then realized who Katie was berat-ing. The burly man, looking absolutely bemused at the tirade he was receiving, was the man who sometimes delivered meat to the inn. He was wearing his usual uniform of green polo shirt and workman-style dark gray trousers. It must be Derek. It hadn't occurred me that the inn would source meat from the same supplier as the manor house, but it made sense we used the same butcher as the one Katie was feuding with.

Katie's voice traveled across the carpark, and now Derek's broad Somerset accent joined her Irish tones. They were talking over each other, a tirade of angry dissonance, of outrage.

"You're a gobdeen!" Katie shouted.

Derek laughed in her face. "What does that even mean?"

"It means, *you*—a wheeler dealer, ripping people off, trying to make a profit at anyone's cost. You could peel an orange in your pocket."

"Ark et ye—you're not even making sense."

"I'm not making sense?" Katie yelled. "Talk about pot and kettle. What you think passes as a decent sausage doesn't make sense."

"Ye ought to be careful, mind. Yelling at me in a public space, shouting your head off about sausages. People round 'ere will think you've lost your marbles. If you had any to begin with, that is."

Katie appeared to calm down. She looked to be taking one deep breath after another. But I soon realized her outspokenness had been replaced with quiet, red-hot fury. "It's gone way further than sausages. You have to speak to the police and tell them I'd sent the notes to you. I know you received them. They were never intended for the earl, God rest his soul."

"What notes? You really are going round the twist. You never wrote to me, you daft fool."

"I did!" she shrieked. "I called you evil. Which ye are. And said you wouldn't get away with your thieving practices."

He put down an empty crate and crossed his arm. "Evil, am I? Believe you me, I would have responded to them immediately in kind."

Katie put her hands on her hips. "Well, at least tell them we were in the habit of sending each other insulting notes."

"I will not," he retorted. "What's more, I was planning to stay for a pint. You've put me off my drink." He left in a huff and got back into his delivery van.

I slipped out of sight, not wanting to incur any more of Katie's wrath, but Eve had heard the kerfuffle and emerged from the kitchen.

"Katie," she said, her voice soft and placating. "Mitty is in the bar looking for you."

"Mitty is up and about?" Katie asked. I could visibly see her body calm, the tension in her shoulders dropping, the color of her cheeks receding closer to its usual creamy complexion.

I watched her follow Eve through the back entrance. How quickly Katie mellowed at just the mention of Mitty's name. Meanwhile, my own mood soared. If Mitty was no longer bed-bound, maybe now I'd be able to speak to him about the past.

I followed at a discreet distance, making my way to the inn's front door. I gave Katie a few minutes to settle and then entered the bar, where I saw Katie and Mitty sitting at a table holding hands. I stood behind a pillar and hoped that they wouldn't look in my direction.

It was such a sweet sight, the two friends talking gently in that intimate way that comes from years of knowing one another and genuine mutual affection. And, just maybe, it was more than a platonic connection. Katie was asking Mitty about his afternoon, inquiring about what he ate for lunch, if it was enough, should she make a chicken pie for dinner. He answered in simple sentences, clearly still frustrated that his speech wasn't as clear as it had been because of his stroke.

"Don't you worry," she soothed. "That speech therapy is making a world of difference." His voice grew bolder than before. Katie listened, her face attentive, no sign of any frustration. It was a far cry from the angry Katie of minutes ago. I was having trouble reconciling the two Katies—the one who would send those awful notes and this woman, so full of kindness.

As I mused on these two points, Edward came into the bar and went to sit with Mitty and Katie. I felt so torn. I wanted to believe that this sweet older woman, holding hands with the retired gamekeeper, was the real Katie Donegal. Not the irate woman who liked to send threats. Maybe I could confide in Edward later. He worked for the Champneys, after all. He might have insider information. And I needed to get Mitty alone somehow. Argh. There were so many plates spinning, so many lines of inquiry to follow, so many secrets to uncover. I didn't know where to start.

I went to the bar to ask Eve for some coffee. In my experience, coffee always helped.

While Eve poured me a cup of the strong stuff, I asked her if she thought Mitty was recuperating. Eve nodded. "He looks right as rain, don't you think? Maybe Susan's tonics have been working their magic." She winked.

I agreed with Eve. Mitty looked infinitely stronger than the man I'd spoken to at Katie's last week. I took a sip of coffee, letting my palms burn a little on the porcelain cup. I was certain that Mitty knew something about my birth parents. He'd tried to speak to me when I'd visited him. He'd recognized Valerie and said he saw her features in me. And then he had told Katie that I looked like my father. My father! If only I'd been able to get more information from him, but he appeared to lose the thread of his memories. And Katie had blocked me from asking anything more. She had literally talked over him, forcing Susan's tonic down his throat. Why? Was she protecting Mitty? Protecting me? Or was there some other, darker secret she was trying to keep under wraps?

I decided to face Katie's potential wrath and invite myself to sit at their table. No more hanging around, hoping for answers to appear out of thin air. But as I stood from the barstool, DI Hembly and Sgt. Lane strode into the bar and went straight to Katie's table.

"Mrs. Donegal?" DI Hembly asked. "May we speak somewhere privately? We have some more questions for you."

Katie looked panicked. Mitty and Edward, too. I held my breath, caught between the bar and the restaurant, watching the scene unfurl as if it were a movie.

She went to rise, but Mitty held onto her hands. "Stay." She settled herself again and nodded, seeming to take strength from Mitty.

"I'll stay right where I am. You can say anything you have to say to me in front of my friends."

"Very well," DI Hembly said. The two detectives pulled out chairs and sat. He removed something encased in a clear plastic bag from his knapsack. I squinted. The object was too small to see.

Hembly held the bag in front of Katie. "Does this look familiar?" he asked, his voice even but grave.

Katie stared at the bag. I could see now that it was a long piece of twine, doubled up and curled around itself. She nodded. "It's twine. Of course, it looks familiar. I use kitchen twine at Broomewode Hall nearly every day." She stared at him like he was wasting her time.

"We're going to need you to accompany us to the police station to help with our inquiries."

Katie looked sick but simply nodded and asked Edward to look after Mitty.

"Are you in trouble, Katie?" Mitty asked slowly.

"No, I haven't done anything wrong. Don't you worry. They aren't arresting me, are you?" She looked at DI Hembly with a challenge in her eye.

"No," he said, but I heard the implied *not yet.*

She stood and walked out with the detectives.

I couldn't believe what I'd just witnessed. The detectives thought the earl had been murdered by someone knocking him off his horse with rope or string. That was why the earl had a red mark across his chest. Could simple kitchen twine have really caused such a fatal accident? And did Katie use it to murder her employer?

CHAPTER 17

Shocked, I took a seat at the bar.

Eve looked at me aghast. She pulled at the end of her long braid nervously. "Not Katie," she said softly. "Why, she was the first person in Broomewode to show me kindness when I moved here. She has a good heart. I can feel it." She smoothed down her smock-style T-shirt.

It was upsetting to see Eve disturbed. But I was disturbed too. What was going on?

"Something's off, Poppy," she said. "Do you feel it? As though the energy vortex that draws us here is off-kilter somehow." She sighed deeply. "I wonder if it's safe for us."

At least she was worried about herself as well as me. I was getting tired of these messages telling me to leave. If Eve was worried about her own safety as well as mine, it was better, somehow. Like I wasn't being singled out for the bad stuff. Finally, because she seemed to be worried about both of us, I could contemplate leaving.

"I could visit my parents," I said, surprised that the idea popped into my head. I wondered if I'd been thinking about leaving but hadn't acknowledged my thoughts yet. "They live in the south of France."

"Well, that would be nice. You could have a holiday."

I felt terrible about how long it had been since I visited my mom and dad. Since I'd started the baking show, I knew I'd been distant—too caught up discovering my history to focus properly on the present. But watching how quickly and completely disaster had struck the Champney family, well, it brought home how much I needed to appreciate the parents who had brought me up.

A local man came up and ordered a pint of cider, and Eve busied herself serving him.

When was the last time I'd seen my folks? At least three months. Although I still called them a bunch, it wasn't the same. I pulled out my phone and decided to remedy this icky feeling. With a few presses, I searched my way through the internet to a cheap flight comparison site. My eyes flickered across the options. I could fly into Nice and surprise them. No. They'd rather anticipate my visit. That was half the fun. Dad would organize the sightseeing, and Mom would plan meals.

"What you up to, dearie?" Eve inquired when the man walked away with his pint of cider.

I told her that I'd looked at flights, thinking I'd visit my parents. "Since the show started filming, I've felt tied to Broomewode Village at the weekends. I mean, I've felt tied to this place for many other reasons, too. But maybe getting away for a short break is a good idea."

Eve nodded. "Elspeth, Susan, and I are all worried about you. The tractor accident was most likely just that, but you are too often in the path of harm. I'm glad you've made plans to be elsewhere." She quickly added, "It's different for me. I've been here so long, but there's no denying you do seem to attract danger."

I must have looked glum because Eve quickly added, "We only warn you because we love you. You're our sister. We want you to be safe. And where's safer than with your family? Besides, I can't wait to see what you bring me back as a gift."

I had to smile. Maybe Eve was right. But if she thought I was going to stop searching for my birth parents, then she was wrong. All the way wrong. I looked over to where Mitty and Edward were talking quietly. By his hand gestures, I could tell that Edward was trying to reassure the old game-keeper. Was it strange for Mitty to be sitting in the pub with his successor? He seemed perfectly happy and no doubt could pass on his wisdom to Edward, the new gamekeeper. I hoped so.

The urge to talk to Mitty about my birth dad was over-whelming. I wanted to know who he thought I'd looked like, and I was certain he was lucid enough to tell me, but I hesi-tated. I shouldn't crash Edward and Mitty's bonding time with my own agenda, and yet when might I have a better opportunity?

I was about to head over to their table when I heard my name called. I turned quickly, and there was Benedict, standing in the doorway. He caught my eye and smiled the most genuine warm smile that my stomach flipped. *Oh, Bene-dict.* I was so confused. After what his mother had said, any notions of possible romance felt smashed. But the draw was undeniable. Benedict did something to me. Something that felt just as magical as anything I'd encountered in Broomewode.

"Hi," he said softly. "It's good to see you."

I returned the comment and was surprised as I felt his lips brush against my cheek. He smelled wonderful.

"How are you holding up?" I asked him.

He grimaced. "It's all a bit ghastly. Mother had hysterics when the police insisted on taking Father's body away. I had to call the doctor to her. She hasn't been herself. Now there's all this business with Katie. I don't know if you've heard, but Mother's let her go because of those dreadful notes. I must talk to her. Poor Katie's been with our family since before we came here."

I hated to be the bearer of bad news, but he'd find out soon enough. "Katie was taken away by the police for questioning."

Benedict looked crestfallen. "I knew they were looking for her. I was hoping to talk to her before they found her. I can't understand what's going on."

"I can't quite get my head around it, either," I confessed as Benedict took a seat next to me. Eve offered him a drink, but he thanked her and declined. I gave Eve a hard stare, like get the message already—coven sister or not, a little space, please. And, giving us both a very knowing and embarrassing look, she walked to the other end of the bar, where a frustrated customer was waiting.

Benedict put his head in his hands. It was the first time I'd seen him look so dejected. "This is all a horrible mess. I'm going to make sure that Katie gets a good defense lawyer."

"You mean they think she really did it?"

He raised his head and looked at me sadly. "The evidence is compelling. I'm certain they plan to arrest her for murder after questioning."

"But they pulled out a length of string. If playing with string was suspicious, they'd have to arrest Gateau, my cat."

Benedict managed a smile. "They have a length of kitchen twine that has scrapings of bark on it from the tree near where my father was killed. They found it in her apron pocket. She must have quickly taken it from the tree after my father fell and then run away."

I couldn't believe it. I'd known the odds were stacked against Katie, but not the degree of evidence which the police had found. I was shocked. The sweet woman who looked after Mitty with such love and care? But then I flashed back to the image of Katie arguing with the butcher. She'd been furious. She was stubborn. And loose-tongued. And she obviously had enemies, like the butcher. But I still didn't see her as a killer.

Benedict's response also made zero sense. "If you think she killed your dad, why offer to pay for her defense?"

"Whatever happened yesterday, I'm certain Katie didn't mean to kill him. No doubt she was angry and wanted to hurt him, but the Katie I know would never kill anyone."

I understood his feelings. Katie must be like a second mother to him—or primary mother, given the countess's cold nature.

I'd been thinking about the logistics, too. "How would Katie even have managed it? She'd have had to race to the spot where the earl was killed and recover her twine, all while cooking breakfast for fifty people." It didn't seem possible.

"You're forgetting that she went to the cellar to fetch wine. Don't you remember the door was open? She had staff helping her cook the breakfast. Who'd have noticed if she took a few extra minutes in the cellar? The police timed it. It was possible."

I asked what would happen to Mitty with Katie gone, and he promised that Mitty would be properly looked after. "There's no need for him to leave Katie's cottage. I'll make sure there's someone around to give him the care he needs."

"That's good." I felt suddenly awkward. He seemed momentarily tongue-tied too. Then he said, "Look, about what my mother said to you—"

Before he could finish that most interesting sentence, there was a burst of noise, and the three bakers rushed into the pub, talking at the top of their lungs.

"My God, what a relief," Florence was saying.

"I thought I was going to fade away in there," Gaurav said. "I was turning into a saucepan of melted chocolate."

"Och, tell me about it," Hamish grumbled. "Why why why do they film this show in warm weather? How are we supposed to control baking temperatures?"

"It's like they torture us on purpose," Florence said. "It's a nightmare. I'm certain my makeup was running down my face. I was sweating like I was running a marathon."

"The show *is* a marathon," Gaurav added.

Benedict raised his eyebrows and smiled. "It's almost nice to hear such normal grumblings. No deception. No death." He leaned a bit closer. "I'll catch up with you later. Go find out how today went for your friends. I'm going to take Mitty back to the cottage. Edward can help."

Before I could answer, Florence caught sight of us, formed her perfect lips into an *O* when she saw who I was talking to, and rushed over.

"Your Lordship," she said in a grandiose voice usually reserved for a film crew. "I'm so sorry for your loss."

"That's very kind of you," Benedict replied. I imagined he'd said those words a hundred times since his father's death. "And please, call me Ben. I'm not ready to assume my father's title quite yet."

Florence flushed. "No, of course. If there's anything I can do..."

She trailed off.

"I'll keep that in mind." He turned and looked at me. There was a hint of humor in his eyes. Perhaps he was accustomed to people sucking up to him because of his title and wealth. Now that he was the Earl of Frome, it would be worse. The airs and graces Florence put on around the Champneys was kind of excruciating.

"Talk to you later, Poppy," Benedict said quietly.

"Goodbye, Ben," Florence called in her most flirtatious tone.

She grabbed my arm the second he walked away and pulled me over to where the two remaining bakers were pouring a bottle of white wine. I was scared that she was going to tease me about having an obvious tête-à-tête with Benedict, but to my relief, she was too caught up with her own day. "Did you watch us, Poppy?" she asked. "Did you come?"

I laughed and told her I'd watched for a little while. "You looked so cool and competent," I told her. "Dare I ask how it went?"

Hamish and Florence both spoke over one another, but once I'd decoded their breathy rundown of the afternoon, I realized Hamish won the signature bake and Gaurav the technical—and Florence came second in both challenges. I looked at her. The sweet as pie façade she'd put on for Benedict had dropped completely. The light had gone out of her eyes. She was worried. Deeply worried. I felt a pang of remorse. Was Florence going to blame me that she hadn't had exclusive use of the Happy Eggs? I shook the thought from my mind. There were more important things to be worrying about.

But it seemed that Florence wasn't the only one who was worried. The moment I pulled up a chair and accepted a cool glass of white wine, the three remaining bakers spun stories of their baking woes. Hamish had trouble tempering his chocolate; Florence had gone to pieces layering her Dobos torte; Gaurav burnt his chocolate caramel sauce and had to start over at the last moment. The competition was still anyone's game. Florence was stressed, though. I could feel the tension coming off her in waves. I remembered what she'd told me about her agent saying she needed to win.

Once they'd calmed down about the day, I asked all three to share their showstopper plans. "Don't be superstitious, guys. It's not like you to withhold like this. The theme is the circus, right? I kind of heard the producers talking about it up at the tent earlier."

Hamish agreed. "I'm sick about it, to be honest. My circus-themed showstopper is a series of thin bûche de Noël with coffee, chocolate, and mascarpone filling, hoisted up to create a kind of tightrope with a biscuit tightrope walker and a chocolate ring of fire flaming beneath. If I've got time, the plan is to make little spectators out of meringue. Oh, and there'll be some peanut butter frosting in there somewhere."

I inhaled. "Wowzers." It sounded magnificent and complicated—exactly what a showstopper should be—but was Hamish mixing too many flavors and textures together? I'd be interested to see how it turned out tomorrow.

"I honestly don't know how I'm going to pull it all off in time," he said, almost reading my mind. "It's crazy to think that four hours is never enough."

Gaurav was next to spill the cocoa beans. "It's my grandma's recipe," he said. We all leaned in a little closer. Florence took a gulp of wine.

"Think lion tamers, lions, in a caramel chocolate grandstand with a marzipan audience. The works. What makes it special is the flavor of the chocolate. I infuse it with cardamon. It tastes out of this world when my grandma does it. But she has, like, magic in her fingertips. It's like she can make the ingredients do her bidding."

I smiled to myself. If only I'd been able to use magic during my time on the show, I'd be in the final—but not through merit! I was sure it wouldn't feel good to use magic to my own gain, however tempting it might be.

While I'd been daydreaming, the group had fallen silent. The faces of my three friends had entirely different expressions. Hamish looked frustrated, Gaurav looked bemused, and Florence—well, Florence looked stubborn. A child holding on to a bag of candy came to mind.

"You're seriously not going to tell us?" Hamish said, a deep crease forming across his forehead.

"We're the three muffin-tiers, remember?" Gaurav said quietly.

"Really?" I added.

Florence crossed her arms. "There's too much riding on tomorrow. I'm not going to jinx it."

My mind flashed back to Florence's petulant fit about the others getting happy eggs. This kind of competitiveness broke with the moral code of the other contestants. We helped each other. We picked one another up when we were down. We shared expertise and advice. This was *not* very *Great British Baking Contest* of Florence. I couldn't help thinking her selfish attitude would bring her bad luck in tomorrow's semifinal.

CHAPTER 18

*T*he next morning I arrived for work in the rain. For the first time this season of *The Great British Baking Contest*, it was going to be raining during filming. Not a cats and dogs downpour, more like a gentle summer shower—it reminded me of a smattering of sprinkles on ice cream. But still, there was something unsettling about the change in weather. The skies were gray, but a summer shower couldn't dampen the excitement of the spectators, of whom I was one. Today was crunch time. We were going to find out which two lucky bakers were going to make it to the final bake-off. And find out who would go home.

From experience (by which I meant rewatching every single episode of the show ever filmed), the final three were the contestants that everyone remembered. Viewers followed them through the weeks, were invested in their journeys, knew their backstories, tried to predict what they'd bake and how well it would turn out. They knew what style of clothes they wore, if they preferred lipstick or collared shirts. They knew the nervous tics: the flick of the hair in distress, the subtle wrist-rolling. The contestants had been living in homes and hearts for weeks.

And now that I was on the outside of the show again, a viewer as opposed to a participant, I felt the same way.

Since this season had been full of misfortune, only two bakers would face each other in the final. I knew my friends felt the extra pressure. As well as cakes, they were making history. In Florence's case, possibly a new career.

It felt almost masochistic to be back at the tent for the semifinal showdown, but I knew I couldn't miss today's big showstopper event. I wasn't part of the action, but my heart was still in that tent. The baking contest was part of me. It had led me to understanding who I was and where I came from. If I hadn't met the great Elspeth Peach, then I would never have known that my powers extended beyond seeing and communicating with ghosts. I would never have known I was a water witch. And if I hadn't realized that about myself, then I would have spent even longer as a stranger to myself, positioned even further away from my birth parents.

Today's crowd was larger than usual, even though filming showstoppers was a long, laborious affair. I guessed they were as eager as I to see who'd come out on top today—even if it meant being almost as exhausted watching the bakers at work as they were themselves. I'd positioned myself up in the front and was surprised to be accosted by several of the onlookers. Even though the show hadn't aired yet, interested locals could come by and watch the filming and one or two recognized me and we chatted about my new role at the inn.

"How exciting," one gray-haired lady said, "to be able to eat the cakes of a real-life contestant. I'll tell all my friends." Inwardly I squirmed, still kicking myself. The last thing I wanted at work was to be recognized from the show and become a kind of tourist attraction. Maybe Eve and Ruta would welcome the extra customers, but that kind of attention was my worst nightmare (beyond dropping cakes onto the floor as I took them out of the oven—that was a nightmare that haunted me weekly).

An older gentleman asked me a series of increasingly probing questions starting with what I most liked to bake and ending with who I thought was going to win. I tried to be as polite as I could muster—the attention was flattering but also embarrassing, and of course, I wasn't going to spill the beans on who I thought would take the crown. I wasn't sure myself. I was happy to explain that actually my favorite thing to bake was a Bakewell tart! There was something so comforting about the almond and cherry combination and a buttery crust. I got hungry only thinking about it. And, as I talked with the group, it dawned on me just how different my life might become once the show aired. I was getting a small taste of what recognition, even fame, felt like—and it was strange.

The last three days had truly taken it out of me, and what with meeting Joanna/not Joanna, having a tractor almost mow me down, a planned and then abandoned date with a man I'd hoped might be more than a friend—oh, yes, and the murder of the Earl of Frome—I'd driven home with Gateau after dinner last night and fallen into bed. Mildred, my kitchen ghost, chastised me for staying away from the house so much. She'd complained it was getting lonely, that there was no one to have a natter with—she'd even missed Gateau's hissing fits (no love lost between ghost and cat). Mildred lamented that I'd been kicked off the show. "At least when yous was worried about the competition, you'd be in here all week cooking all day long, making a terrible mess," she'd said. Trust Mildred to tell me she missed me by criticizing my kitchen decorum along the way. But I indulged her with the gossip from Broomewode, even as she pretended not to stoop so low as to idle chatter.

I dreamed about the hawk. Although the impressive bird of prey only ever seemed to show up when I was in danger, I found myself strangely comforted by his presence. With his lovely plume, the scattering of white on his rich brown body, the cinnamon-red of his tail, his speckled feathers spread out into a wide fan, the sight of him was majestic. I closed my eyes for a moment, remembering the curved shape of his beak, those dark, sharp eyes of his and the shrill warning call that alerted me to trouble. In my dream, he flew much lower than I'd ever seen in real life. So close, I could see the softness of his feathers, the way the wind rippled through them, and a look of concentration on his face that seemed more human than bird. He wanted to tell me something, but I didn't understand his series of shrill cries. I was desperate for him to speak to me in English, and in the dream I felt that he might do exactly that. Then, of course, I woke up just as his beak was opening for the final time. I couldn't help but wonder if this was my dad's spirit, trying to connect with me in dreams. I wanted to tell him that I hadn't given up. That a plan was coming together to find his true identity. That I was certain Mitty held the key. That I was closer to understanding where my birth mom Valerie was and that somehow I had a hunch that Katie Donegal was in the center of all this. I just had to tie the loose threads together.

I was so lost in my thoughts that I wouldn't have even noticed that Arty had called the final five-minute countdown if it hadn't been for the surge of excitement rippling through the crowd of spectators.

I focused my attention on the tent and saw that Hamish was struggling to put the final touches to his tremendous circus scene. As predicted, he had taken on too much and was fussing with his meringue spectators. Even from afar, I could tell they were too big for his scene.

Gaurav looked neutral—not calm, not frenzied. He was already finished. It was like he'd done his best and he knew he didn't have any more to give.

Florence was focused, bent over her showstopper, putting all the pieces she'd been working on so carefully together at the final moments. She was cutting it fine. But when she pulled back, I could see the full extent of her hard work in all its glory. And it *was* glorious. In fact, it was the most beautiful, expressive and impressive showstopper I'd ever seen. No wonder she'd kept it close to her chest. Unlike Gaurav and Hamish with their modern interpretations, Florence had gone old-school circus. On the left side of a chocolate board, full of white chocolate squares made to look like old-fashioned tiles, was a huge chocolate and caramel lion, roaring. How she had managed that in cake form, I'd no idea. It must have taken a physicist to work out the mathematics of it actually staying up. Next to the gorgeous animal was a lion tamer complete with what must be a spun sugar whip. On the other side of the board was a beautiful elephant with a gorgeous flame-haired woman sitting astride it—probably made from marzipan. Like the lion, it was remarkably lifelike, the skin made with what I assumed must be some kind of white chocolate ganache enhanced by a shimmering silver food dye. It had been painted with exquisite detail, and I realized (foolishly, really, considering how long I'd known Florence) that her skill for making up her face extended to all brush-work, including food. But she had never attempted something this intricate before, which led me to think this was a lightbulb moment—to apply all that she knew about beauty to her cakes and hone her skills painting with food dye and cake brushes. If all this wasn't enough, the *pièce de résistance* was in the center of the board: a woman in a box, ready to be sawn in half—or, in this case, cut in half by the judges. *Bravo, Florence.* Very, very clever. And, of course, the woman bore a keen resemblance to Florence herself.

When Jilly called time, Florence stepped away from her masterpiece, flushed and excited. Hamish and Gaurav looked concerned.

As a viewer at home, and now outside the tent, something happened inside me whenever I watched the part of the show where the contestants had to take their final bakes to the judging table. It was an all-body, physical reaction. I felt their tension in every muscle. Now that I'd been through this ordeal myself, the feeling was even worse.

I stepped closer, right to the limits of the area, ready to hear the judging. I felt anticipation and dread, so nervous for my friends, knowing they couldn't all win but wishing they could. But as Jonathon and Elspeth commented on, and cut into, each showstopper, what I already suspected became clear. Hamish's tasted great but the presentation was sloppy —too rushed. Not a bad word could be said about Florence's bake. "Delicious and breathtaking," Elspeth said. "A masterpiece," Jonathon added. But the surprise came when Gaurav's turn arrived. "This looks sumptuous," Elspeth said, "and there is a lot of skill displayed here…"

I held my breath. I knew Elspeth, and there was a but coming.

"But the chocolate is very bitter in places. It's not balanced. I love the flavor of cardamom, but it's lost in this chocolate. I would have used a lower cocoa percentage, something creamier."

Gaurav's face dropped, and I could feel his pain. He'd hoped to do justice to his grandma's recipe, but alas—Elspeth wasn't impressed.

The judges excused themselves to decide on who was going to win and who was going home.

The crowd around me erupted into excited chatter the second the cameras stopped. It was so strange to be among them, listening to their various speculations, favorites to win. I realized this would have been happening while I was still a contestant and once again reminded myself I was going to need some seriously thick skin once the show began to air.

In what seemed like too short a time, the judges returned, and the cameras began rolling again. The three bakers were solemn, awaiting judgment.

"It was such a close call," Jonathon said. "In fact, in all the time I've been on the show, I don't think I've witnessed a closer semifinal."

"But there could only be one winner," Elspeth continued.

"And one person we have to send home," Jonathon added.

Argh, my heart couldn't take it. I wanted to cover my eyes and ears.

"This part of the show never fails to make me ache with sadness," Elspeth said. "And today, the person we are sending home is a person with a heart of gold. A quiet, kind person who we have all dearly loved getting to know. That person is Gaurav."

There was a gasp from the bakers and crowd alike. Hamish and Florence instantly circled Gaurav in a giant hug.

But it wasn't over yet.

"Our winner this week," Jonathon said, "and of *The Great British Baking Contest's* semifinal, wowed us both with their innovation, skill, and artistic flair. Congratulations, Florence!"

I inwardly whooped and cheered as the bakers, judges, and presenters all clapped. Florence had worked unbelievably hard and got what she wanted. I was pleased for her as much as I was sad to see Gaurav go. I couldn't believe I was going to have to say goodbye to Gaurav. He'd been an amazing contestant, quietly consistent, growing stronger and more confident each week. While others courted the camera (no need to mention names here), Gaurav studied and bettered his techniques, applying his methodical and analytical brain to whatever the judges threw at him—soda bread, cheesecake, scone. He'd been an amazing ally over the weeks, and not only in the baking tent. His background in data analysis proved indispensable when sleuthing became necessary.

I was going to miss him. I'd have a word with Ruta later and ask her to cook up something special this evening for Gaurav's leaving dinner. He'd been very quietly seeing a local girl. Maybe those two would get really serious, and I could be the one to make their wedding cake! I chuckled to myself— here I was, making a stealthy plan for Gaurav's return to the village when he hadn't even left yet.

The contestants had finished hugging one another. All

three had emotion in their eyes. I could see that Florence's were full of happy tears, Hamish's twinkle spoke of relief, and Gaurav had a blank, sad look. The realization that it had all come to an end. He was smiling, though—maybe he was just as relieved as Hamish, except relieved to be out of the competition, not still in it. As good as Gaurav was, I never got the impression that it was super important for him to win. He just enjoyed baking at the weekends, improving his technique.

The bakers were ushered out of the tent by series producer Donald Friesen to have their photograph taken for the *Broomewode News.* He was herding them almost like Sly with the sheep, desperate for them to be captured in the throes of their varying emotions. I spotted Trim immediately, poised and ready to get the shot. I waved and cheered as my three friends emerged onto the grass. I was so incredibly proud and desperate to squeeze them all, but show duties called. I'd see them after the photoshoot.

CHAPTER 19

*a*s I left the visitors' area, I spotted Benedict near the lake, headed my way.

My mood suddenly shifted as I was reminded of all the loose ends I'd yet to tie up. I made my way to the lake, desperate to know if there had been any progress with Katie Donegal's arrest. Had Benedict secured her a defense lawyer? Nothing was adding up, and I felt the weight of responsibility on my shoulders. I needed to make sense of his father's death, but unlike the other times tragedy had struck Broomewode, this didn't feel like my usual compulsion to get on the case and solve a mystery. If Susan and Eve were right, and part of my powers as a witch was bringing a sense of resolution to the living and dead alike, then this case had something extra about it, something with a deeper, more insistent draw. Could it just be about Benedict? Were my feelings messing with my romantic life?

As I drew closer, he looked pleased to see me, a warmth suffusing his sad eyes, a smile playing around his lips. It was like the sight of me soothed him. Had I ever had that kind of effect on a man before? I mean, a living one, that is?

I told him the big news from the tent, and Benedict seemed genuinely interested, despite everything else.

"It's a shame. I liked Gaurav a lot," he said. "I'm sorry he's going, though not as sorry as I was when I heard you were out of the running."

My cheeks betrayed me in a blush, but then I remembered his mother's warning about suitable women and made myself snap out of it and swiftly changed the subject. Flirting with Benedict was a terrible idea. I shuddered, thinking of all the women who'd be only too pleased to spend time with him. I didn't stand a chance. "What's the news about Katie?" I asked.

He looked perturbed. "She was formally arrested this morning. Her DNA was all over that kitchen twine." He swallowed. "As were fibers from my father's hunting jacket."

Ouch. I hoped he'd hired her a very good lawyer. "There must be something she's not telling us. Why did she hate him so much?"

He shook his head. "I'm as confused as you are. I'd have said Katie would do anything to protect our family. Not kill one of us."

Strange thing was, despite the evidence to the contrary, I felt the same way. "Could there be an innocent explanation?" Like she'd accidentally trussed up the earl in kitchen twine, thinking he was a Sunday roast?

"It's damning evidence. I only wish there were another suspect so the police wouldn't be so certain it was Katie."

"What about Farmer Riley?" I asked. "His runaway tractor

nearly killed me, and there are witnesses to him and your father fighting."

"I've heard," Benedict said, looking puzzled. "But I spoke with Riley myself, and he swears that he left the tractor properly braked and not facing downhill toward the café. The tractor company is looking into the possibility of mechanical failure. The police have interviewed him, but they arrested Katie. I suspect they know more than they're telling us."

He paused, frowned, and then looked like he was debating whether to tell me something.

"What is it?" I asked.

"Katie grew up on a farm in rural Ireland. All through my childhood, she liked to tell me stories of what she got up to when she was my age, and they nearly always involved working with all the machines. She always said she was a better mechanic than her brothers."

A cold sensation coursed through my body. Had I got it all wrong? "Machines like tractors," I said, feeling my expression harden.

"Exactly."

"What if we've been looking at this all wrong? What if they were working *together*? They both had reasons for wanting to hurt your father. Farmer Riley out of spite. He felt as if his livelihood was being disrespected by your father. Katie because she thought she was getting the sack after thirty years of service. So they clubbed together, trying to find a way to get revenge. They settled on destroying his café in a freak accident. But when your father took that in his stride and just called the insurance company, Katie decided to give him a real fright and concocted a booby trap that would give him a scare. Maybe she never intended to kill him. She went a step too far without realizing the consequences."

Benedict began to pace the path beside the river. I followed, struggling to keep up with his long stride. I could see his face working through all the possibilities. Trying to find another explanation. I empathized. If those two had collaborated, then that was two people in Broomewode who took risks with other people's lives. I shivered, thinking about how close I had come to death.

As we walked in silence, I stared into the lake's depth. It was so lovely, so undisturbed by everything that was going on around it, by the drizzling clouds and the overcast sky. The swans were as serene and elegant as ever, the water lilies and cattails freshened by drops of rain. A few green-headed mallards ducked for food, their fluffy behinds sticking out of the water. I stayed there for a moment, watching the water's surface, remembering the first vision I'd ever had, and then each subsequent one, telling me something new but never the full story. Suddenly, I started. Was the water moving? Rippling like it was agitated, like it wanted to move more freely? It couldn't be, surely. I wasn't alone. The last thing I needed was another magical occurrence I had to ignore for fear of looking like I was out of my mind.

Benedict coughed, and we came to a standstill.

"About our date," he said, running a hand through his hair.

Okay. Unexpected change of subject.

I nodded, waiting for him to continue. He seemed to hesitate as though about to deliver bad news. I didn't want any more bad news today. I decided that I'd no intention of letting Benedict finish that sentence. I couldn't bear to hear another word about my unsuitability. It was going to take me some time to get over the cruelty of the countess's comments.

Before he could let me down more gently than his mother had, I spoke. "I perfectly understand that you need to think about your new position as earl. And, like your mother said, date more suitable women. Women of your class," I couldn't resist adding. "You don't need to explain."

But to my surprise, Benedict looked irritated.

"No, Poppy. You've got it all wrong. My mother, she has some antiquated notions, but I do not share them. It took me weeks to work up the courage to ask you out. I'm not giving up now. I'm still me. It doesn't matter if I'm the earl or the garden help. I'm the same person. And I don't care if you're the queen of food TV or the woman who makes the cakes at the inn. It's you I care about."

He finally held my gaze, and his brown eyes opened wide. He looked vulnerable.

I couldn't believe it. Did Benedict really like me that much? Was he willing to go against the countess's wishes and get involved with a lowly baker? Surely that wouldn't go down well.

Benedict laughed. "I can see your mind whirring. But please, trust me on this. I know a good thing when I see one. And you, you are good, Poppy Wilkinson, through and through. From that stubborn nature of yours down to innate kindness. I see it." He stopped and took my hands. My heart was skipping through all of its beats—one after another came in a giant rush of feeling. "I see it," he repeated the words with emphasis.

His hands were warm and reassuring. My skin felt so good against his.

He leaned in, cupped my face in his hands, and, all soft lips and tenderness, he kissed me.

But when I opened my eyes, I swore I saw the silhouette of my mother disappear from the water's surface.

❧

Thank you for reading *Cakes and Pains!* I hope you enjoyed it. Poppy's adventures in competition baking, and murder, continue in *Whisk and Reward.* Read a sneak peek below...

❧

Whisk and Reward, Chapter 1

A LIGHT DRIZZLE descended on Broomewode Village on Thursday evening, and by the following morning, the rain had gathered speed and volume and the wind blew great billowing sheets of cool water across the sky. Birds tumbled around clouds, and trees shook their leafy tops. "Thoroughly miserable," I complained to Gateau as we drove along the familiar winding lanes that connected Norton St. Philip to Broomewode. She mewled in reply, shifting in the passenger seat to curl into a tighter ball.

My sweet familiar loathed the rain as much as I did. We made a sorry pair. Both of us had been up all night as the summer storm reached a crescendo. She'd scampered around the entire cottage, annoying Mildred, my kitchen ghost, and keeping me awake. Not that I would have had much luck sleeping anyway. This morning was the Earl of Frome's funeral, and I'd been trying to piece together the strange circumstances of his death. I couldn't believe that Katie Donegal, faithful servant to the earl's family for decades, was a murderer, despite the evidence local police detectives had collected.

Katie had been arrested and charged with the earl's murder, causing more shock in Broomewode. I was worried, too, about the earl's son, Benedict. So many responsibilities had been placed on his shoulders overnight, and he was going to have to stay strong today and put on a brave face as his father was laid to rest in front of the village. My heart ached for him.

Actually, my heart just ached. After a rocky start, Benedict had become special to me. And I to him. I still tingled all over when I recalled the passionate kiss we'd shared. Our kiss had changed everything. I was all topsy-turvy, as Mildred had so helpfully pointed out. Dreaming over the stove, dropping my baking utensils. I didn't seem to know my left from my right anymore. If this was what romance did to a girl, well, I could live without the side effects.

It was a difficult time for a budding romance, though. Benedict had been busy with funeral preparations and comforting his mother. For my part, I'd been kept more than busy with extra shifts at the inn. Pavel, the sous-chef, had caught a horrible stomach bug and taken two days off work to recover. Ruta, the head chef, needed all hands on deck to keep the pub's restaurant afloat. Luckily, we weren't fully booked, but it was enough to exhaust a girl.

Now that Pavel was fully recovered, Ruta had given me the day off to go to the funeral and support Benedict. I hadn't breathed a word of our kiss to anyone but Gateau and Mildred (both great secret-keepers, for obvious reasons), but

Ruta seemed to sense how important it was for me to be there.

I knew there was going to be a big turnout. Not because the earl was a popular man (he rubbed far too many people the wrong way) but because he was the Earl of Frome. Besides, curiosity would get the better of many people. Broomewode was a small, close-knit community, and his death was a momentous rupture to the way things were run around here. The earl was landlord to many people, an integral part of the traditions that bound the villagers together. Whether you liked the guy or not, you couldn't get away from the earl's impact on daily village life. It was strange to think that big personality was gone.

As I turned into Church Lane, the rain showed no signs of letting up. It wasn't cold, just miserable, and I longed for the sun to make an appearance and brighten this solemn day.

The number of cars on the road doubled the closer I got to the church, and I soon found myself crawling along at a snail's pace, desperately trying to find a good place to park. No doubt a lot of Robert Champney's posh friends had driven here for the occasion. No doubt most of those he'd invited to his final, ill-fated hunt last weekend would be here to pay their final respects.

Gateau roused herself, done with napping, and watched the rain as it tapped against the window. As I found a space my little Renault Clio could just squeeze into, nerves kicked in. My body felt alien to me. I wondered if this was another example of witchiness that I'd never paid attention to before. I was beginning to believe I picked up on people's emotions and on atmosphere more than most. Or maybe it was just a sad day. I'd dressed for mourning. I never usually wore black, certainly not from head to toe, and the simple shift dress my best friend Gina had lent me for the occasion didn't quite suit my shape. It was too long in the waist, too tight on the shoulders. I undid my seat belt and took a quick glance in the overhead mirror. A minimal makeup job had seemed the most modest approach to the day, and I'd blow-dried my brown hair straight so it hung past my shoulders. Maybe that was a mistake. Even a few curls would have felt less solemn.

Gateau meowed loudly.

"Come on, then," I said. "Let's do this."

Order your copy today! *Whisk and Reward* is Book 9 in the Great Witches Baking Show series.

A Note from Nancy

Dear Reader,

Thank you for reading *The Great Witches Baking Show* series. I am so grateful for all the enthusiasm this series has received. If you enjoyed Poppy's adventures, you're sure to enjoy the *Village Flower Shop,* the *Vampire Knitting Club*, and the *Vampire Book Club* series.

I hope you'll consider leaving a review and please tell your friends who like cozy mysteries and culinary adventures.

Review on Amazon, Goodreads or BookBub. It makes such a difference.

Join my newsletter for a free prequel, *Tangles and Treasons*, the exciting tale of how the gorgeous Rafe Crosyer was turned into a vampire.

I hope to see you in my private Facebook Group. It's a lot of fun. www.facebook.com/groups/NancyWarrenKnitwits

Turn the page for Poppy's recipe for perfect Madeleines.

Until next time,
Happy Reading,
Nancy

POPPY'S RECIPE FOR PERFECT MADELEINES

This recipe will keep quite happily in the fridge for up to twenty-four hours and makes exactly twenty-four madeleines!

Ingredients:

- 135g salted butter (1/2 cup)
- 30ml honey (2 tbsp)
- 3 large eggs (Happy Eggs are the best!)
- 110g caster sugar (1/2 cup superfine sugar, though regular granulated sugar will work)
- 15g soft light brown sugar (1 ½ tbsp)
- 135g self-raising flour (one generous cup of all-purpose flour with 1 ½ tsp baking powder)
- 10g butter for greasing your madeleine tin (1 tbsp)
- 10g flour for dusting your madeleine tin (1 tbsp)

Method:

1. First up, you have to make sure you have an airtight container big enough to fit your madeleine mix. Got it? Great, now put to one side.

2. Next, grab a medium-sized saucepan and combine the butter and honey, stirring as the two melt together. Once the lumps are gone, take the pan off the heat and leave to cool slightly.

3. Now it's time for some elbow grease or, if you're like me, a little sitting-back-and-watching-my-machine-do-the-work time. Whisk the eggs and sugars together for about ten minutes by hand or until the mix has tripled in volume. The air here is key.

4. Once you've got that volume sorted, fold in the sifted flour and melted butter but go slow and gentle so as not to deplete the egg mix. Once all the ingredients are incorporated, pour into your airtight container and leave it to rest for three hours. If I could, this would be the time I'd go for a pedicure or a nice iced late.

5. Now it's time to grease your madeleine moulds with butter. Once they look slick, lightly dust them with flour – tapping off any excess. Preheat your oven to 180c fan or 190c if not. (375 degrees Fahrenheit)

6. Place a dessert spoon of the mixture in each mould but do be careful not to overfill as the mix will spread out nicely as soon as it hits that lovely warm oven.

7. Bake for twelve – fourteen minutes until golden brown.

Best enjoyed warm with a lovely pot of hot coffee and with a group of your closest friends. Get eating!

Bon appétit!

ALSO BY NANCY WARREN

The best way to keep up with new releases, plus enjoy bonus content and prizes is to join Nancy's newsletter at NancyWarrenAuthor.com or join her in her private Facebook group www.facebook.com/groups/NancyWarrenKnitwits

The Great Witches Baking Show: Culinary Cozy Mystery

The Great Witches Baking Show - Book 1

Baker's Coven - Book 2

A Rolling Scone - Book 3

A Bundt Instrument - Book 4

Blood, Sweat and Tiers - Book 5

Crumbs and Misdemeanors - Book 6

A Cream of Passion - Book 7

Cakes and Pains - Book 8

Whisk and Reward - Book 9

Gingerdead House - A Holiday Whodunnit

The Great Witches Baking Show Boxed Set: Books 1-3

The Great Witches Baking Show Boxed Set: Books 4-6 (includes bonus novella)

The Great Witches Baking Show Boxed Set: Books 7-9

Vampire Knitting Club Boxed Set: Books 7-9

Vampire Knitting Club Boxed Set: Books 10-12

Vampire Book Club: Paranormal Women's Fiction Cozy Mystery

Crossing the Lines - Prequel

The Vampire Book Club - Book 1

Chapter and Curse - Book 2

A Spelling Mistake - Book 3

A Poisonous Review - Book 4

Abigail Dixon: A 1920s Cozy Historical Mystery

In 1920s Paris everything is très chic, except murder.

Death of a Flapper - Book 1

Toni Diamond Mysteries

Toni is a successful saleswoman for Lady Bianca Cosmetics in this series of humorous cozy mysteries.

Frosted Shadow - Book 1

Ultimate Concealer - Book 2

Midnight Shimmer - Book 3

A Diamond Choker For Christmas - A Holiday Whodunnit

Toni Diamond Mysteries Boxed Set: Books 1-4

The Almost Wives Club: Contemporary Romantic Comedy

An enchanted wedding dress is a matchmaker in this series of romantic comedies where five runaway brides find out who the best men really are!

Take a Chance: Contemporary Romance

Meet the Chance family, a cobbled together family of eleven kids who are all grown up and finding their ways in life and love.

For a complete list of books, check out Nancy's website at NancyWarrenAuthor.com

ABOUT THE AUTHOR

Nancy Warren is the USA Today Bestselling author of more than 100 novels. She's originally from Vancouver, Canada, though she tends to wander and has lived in England, Italy and California at various times. While living in Oxford she dreamed up The Vampire Knitting Club. Favorite moments include being the answer to a crossword puzzle clue in Canada's National Post newspaper, being featured on the front page of the New York Times when her book Speed Dating launched Harlequin's NASCAR series, and being nominated three times for Romance Writers of America's RITA award. She has an MA in Creative Writing from Bath Spa University. She's an avid hiker, loves chocolate and most of all, loves to hear from readers!

The best way to stay in touch is to sign up for Nancy's newsletter at NancyWarrenAuthor.com or www.facebook.com/groups/NancyWarrenKnitwits

To learn more about Nancy and her books
NancyWarrenAuthor.com

Made in the USA
Middletown, DE
09 July 2023